ZOMBIE SHARKS WITH METAL TEETH

ZOMBIE SHARKS WITH METAL TEETH

Stories

STEPHEN GRAHAM JONES

OPEN ROAD

INTEGRATED MEDIA
NEW YORK

ISBN: 979-8-3372-0093-4

This edition published in 2025 by Open Road Integrated Media, Inc.
180 Maiden Lane
New York, NY 10038
www.openroadmedia.com

for my brother Tommy

and for William Colton Hughes

CONTENTS

CONTENTS

LET'S SEE WHAT HAPPENS: AN INTRODUCTION

by Jeremy Robert Johnson

Welcome to Open Swim Hour at the ZOMBIE SHARKS WITH METAL TEETH Recreation Center. We hope you enjoy Stephen Graham Jones' newest interactive exhibit of oddities (aquamarine and otherwise).

Go ahead—dip a toe in the water and watch the ripples spread. Or get your courage up and dive right in, heedless of what might be waiting for you below the surface. Others have done it. They signed the waiver too. So go for it.

Or you can finish this quick orientation. Let me have a second of your time to tell you what you're about to get into, and what kind of mind would create the book that inspired a place like this. Maybe your odds of survival crawl upwards.

Maybe.

Or maybe the longer we wait and chat, the hungrier these things get. You never know.

You'll stick around?

Fantastic. Here's what I know about the book and its author:

Zombie Sharks with Metal Teeth is like zero other books by Stephen Graham Jones. Which also means that it is—in its startling idiosyncrasy—like every book in his catalog. Which is to further say that Stephen Graham Jones has made the noble, ever-insane choice to be a Writer, genres-be-damned (or lovingly embraced, or mutilated, or all of the above).

This is a hard row to hoe, being a Writer. It lacks the comfort of being a genre-specific ham-n-egger, grinding out comfort food with AC/DC dependability. There's no built-in marketing platform for the Writer, no easy answers for bookshop owners when they're wondering where the hell to shelve your new meta-fictional crime memoir. And you've got to create an audience by sheer will, prolificacy, and the strength of your voice. You have to hope there are readers out there brave enough to follow you down whatever strange roads may call.

Jones is nowhere near the first to attempt such a mad endeavor—genre-and-format-jumping folks like Joyce Carol Oates, Dan Simmons, and Joe R. Lansdale have built amazing careers and followings by combining a sterling work ethic with fearless talent. They were brave enough to do what they wanted, and they were great enough to make it look like a sure-footed ascent, even in the deeply strange territories of *Bellefleur* or *The Terror* or *Bubba Ho-Tep*. And it must be these precedents that gave Jones the courage to unleash *Zombie Sharks with Metal Teeth*, his weirdest, wildest book to date.

Much like the mad-but-brilliant scientists in this collection's titular story, Jones has created the tales here with experimental glee, yielding an astonishing assortment of mutated manuscripts.

The investigational "Let's see what happens" mentality at play in this collection means that the story about gigantic soul-storing moon-shrimp will also be told by a dime store P.I. It means that elderly love and parenting are monster-mashed to deeper meaning. It means Kafka goes corporate inspector, basset hounds get sexy, and the aliens are popping up everywhere. It means you'll get your Raymond Carver via dog food therapy and the Please-Let-It-Just-Fucking-Die world of zombie fiction gets repurposed twice in beautifully heart-rending ways. And yeah, there are hamsters.

I'll just say it—Jones went off the deep end this time. But it's thrilling to watch an artist dive into their mind's Marianas Trench and return with exploding oceanic oddities—Coltrane going from devilish smooth to full-stellar squonk, Aphex Twin going from ambient pharmacist to robot brain-masher. And here: Intrepid Writer Stephen Graham Jones going from the assured, human horror of earlier collection *The Ones Who Got Away* to the outstanding aberrations of *Zombie Sharks with Metal Teeth*.

The How or Why of our decision to actualize *Zombie Sharks with Metal Teeth* as a Rec Center eludes me. Perhaps we were infected by Jones' mad momentum. Our own moment of "Let's See What Happens."

But here we are, Dearest/Bravest Reader, and you are now present for Stephen Graham Jones's most awesomely outré exhibit of previously unimagined aquatic life forms. Sure, the sharks are deadlier than ever and the crustaceans have gone Brobdingnagian, but trust me, the water's . . .

Honestly, the water's really fucked up too. That rainbow oil-slick on the surface can't be good for you. No guarantees—you might come out of there short a limb, or a dearly held tenet of reality. Jones was supposed to be your lifeguard, but he's already left here to walk some new dark road, and now you're alone with the weird, wet things.

Really, it was your fault for trusting a Writer—the best of them are devious shapeshifters, and Jones has more skins and voices than we know.

C'est la vie. Head on in. Mind the undertow.

Good Luck and Happy Swimming!

The Sleep of Reason Produces Monsters

—GOYA

. . . after this there was only common experience
—CLIVE BARKER

GOOD TIMES

So one day you're there on the couch doing nothing pretty much, just petting your dog Sheila and shaking you head at J.J. on the television, and then during a commercial for soap you follow your arm down to see what your hand's up to, and there are your fingers, rolling one of your basset hound's thick leathery nipples back and forth.

Do you stop all at once or slow down, let your hand just move back to her side like nothing's happened here? Nothing at all.

And her name isn't really Sheila either, of course. Nobody would name a dog built like her anything but Cleo, or Tilda.

But, Sheila.

She's been gone now for six weeks and five days.

Don't say her name out loud, quietly.

Okay, don't say it again.

Just move your hand away from the dog slowly, all one petting motion.

Any moment now.

Just a little longer though, maybe.

Draw the curtains if you have to.

THE AGE OF HASTY RETREATS

These were the days when, if you wanted to survive, you wore a leather or canvas belt, with loops spaced evenly all around it, loops made from shoestrings. You could find the shoestrings everywhere. Every husk of a person lying in the streets, all of them who hadn't been caught in the shower or doing yoga, they had some kind of footwear on them.

And of course you target the men, because they have laces more often. You don't so much want the workboot kind of lace, though; they're unforgiving, can get you killed. No, what you need are the kind that will break away with a flick of your wrist. And, if you're not sure, then it never hurts to go ahead and cut that loop maybe halfway through, just to be sure. If it snaps too early, while you're scrambling over a burnt car, diving through a window, then so be it. Like I said, there are shoes everywhere.

As for the belt itself, though, you need something wide. A general rule of thumb is that, if it fits through the loops of your pants, then it's not sturdy enough. And, anyway, that belt's going to be carrying maybe thirty pounds of lifesaving for you, and asking it to do that while *not* pulling your pants down, tripping you up, that's maybe too much, think?

The kind of belt you want, that works best, it's the kind that's made *not* to go through the loops. Police officers' are the best bet, though, to avoid the inevitable creaking, you'll either have to keep them oiled or just ditch all the superhero utility pouches you're already falling in love with. But, mace, pepper spray—you really think the undead care about their eyes? Not that a pistol isn't a good idea, in spite of the attention it'll draw, but, if you've got a pistol, then carry that pistol at all times. It's no good in the holster. And of course always save one round for yourself.

But, since the majority of the police force went down in the first day or two, protecting and serving, you might want to check behind the seats or in the toolboxes of the pickup trucks parked around construction sites. Toolbelts. They're supple, always already broken in. Just cut or chew the pouches off, adjust the buckle so the belt rides on your hips like a real gunslinger, and you're ready. Or, as soon as you poke holes (coat hangers work) for the loops of shoe strings, then all that's left is to raid the pantries, crack open the cat food. It works for all the little animals except squirrels, but who would want a squirrel?

No, domestics are the best, by far. With a single can of cat food, you can often draw in a full load, completely recharge your belt. The zombies can't catch them, the dogs, the cats, so they're everywhere, hiding, starving. Just wanting some companionship. Which you can of course provide.

And, sure, let them eat if you want. It'll make them trust you, maybe even enough that you can pick them up.

As for size, under ten pounds is best, six is about ideal. Next is the hard part: working those small bodies into the loops you've fashioned onto your belt. And never by the neck. What use would it be to carry around a cat or lapdog you've strangled? That'd be sick, and anyway, zombies don't like dead flesh. Looping them under the armpits is best. Granted, it leaves their hind legs free to pedal a furrow into your leg or buttocks, but there are ways around that. You can tie their feet together, of course, or just break them, whatever you're comfortable with. However, if there's blood from that break, then you've spoiled the cat, the puppy (and iguanas are useless, might as well be dead as far as zombies are concerned). Start over, do it right this time. Your life depends on it. And, yes, hopefully you won't need to use these 'grenades' you're making, but of course, in a more ideal world, the dead wouldn't be walking either, right? Right.

So, with a full, squirming belt, then just go about living in your usual manner, and, whenever it happens—and it will—that you're making your mad dash away from whatever horde you've stumbled onto, and they're gaining like they always do, then all you have to do is, without breaking stride, pull on the cat or puppy by whatever your dominant hand is, and splash it down onto the ground. The idea is that you want some of that blood in the air. And, if you've broken this pet's legs, then of course the lead zombie (there's always a runner) will be on it in a flash, its maw buried in the gore, and if you've tied them together, then it's pretty much the same result.

And, yes, some survivors have rigged complicated loops that both break away *and* untie the pet's legs at the same time, thus giving the zombies a *moving*, though gratefully injured distraction, but these knots, all that string—do you really want to trust your escape to whether or not you went under or over before you pulled tight?

What you need, of course, it's a dog or cat that *can't* run. Which, yes, starvation will to some degree satisfy, but most of us carry odd bits of food for the animals. Because we care about them? I don't think that's completely it, no. And it's not a thank you in advance either, not really. It's more that the animals have conditioned us to feed them. Or—by feeding them just enough to keep them alive, we're demonstrating that we still have some tether, no matter how bloody, to the old world. To the way it was.

And it would be completely dishonest of me to try to say that all of us don't hitch the belts around such that our favorite animal is at our dominant hand. The hand we most like to pet with. That connection with a palm-sized skull, a warm body, one dependent upon you, one happy that you're touching it, it can get you through a whole night of hiding behind a mailbox, if you need it to. Though of course most in that situation will break, will start lobbing pets into the street like mortars, perhaps kissing each on the mouth before slinging it up into the sky. And then others, of course, after expending half their belt, will slide to their knees on the asphalt, unbuckle, and release their dogs and cats, try to shoo them away before the horde overwhelms them. If you want to live, however, then you'll empty belt after belt behind you.

There's even legend of a tall man, our progenitor perhaps, who wears bandoliers across his chest, a suckling kitten thumbed into each cartridge space, a bottle of milk in his pocket to keep them alive.

And, yes, with the cats at least, you can sling them by the tail before release if you want—the sound they make is perfect—but you have to time it just right, so the cat sails over the horde's heads, and you also have to never reconsider, never stop swinging, because that's a cat you'll never reholster. What's sad is to have somebody return from a scavenging mission unscathed by the dead but with their eye clawed out, soon to be infected. We don't have enough people for those kinds of mistakes.

As for the animals—is this not why we domesticated them? For companionship in times of leisure, sure, but, in times like this, to serve us, to help us survive. They die fully aware of what their sacrifice means, are proud to be allowing us another few feet of life.

However, there are of course lines.

The second day of the plague, when it spilled down from the airport, infected downtown, my neighbor's nine-year-old son attempted to mask his scent with the gore of a decapitated zombie. A fully effective measure, provided you have the nerve, the stomach—he had both—but you don't want to let that gore come into contact with your tear ducts, or any cuts you might have.

Things progressed in the predictable way after that, until my neighbor took the easy way out: siphoned the gas from his car, lawnmower, and weedeater, and set fire to himself and his son. Valiant, perhaps, but irresponsible as well. He didn't take into account the acetylene torch in his garage.

When the flames spread there, as flames will, the resulting explosion caved in the wall of *my* son's bedroom, crushing his right leg while he slept. Luckily it's a closed break, no bone coming through the skin, but of course pushing him around in a wheelchair or shopping cart, even strapped to a dolly or pulled in a make-do rickshaw, that's no way to beat a hasty retreat. And this is the age of hasty retreats.

Luckily for *me*, though, he's small for his age—six—so I've been able to fashion a quiver of sorts for him to ride in. He sits backwards, of course, to better see (and warn me about) our constant pursuers, and, all in all, it's not bad. I always know where he is, and, as for him, he's named the animals I wear around my belt. There's Axel and Win and Lobby and General Tough and Red Eye and, after his mother, Sidney.

And so we scavenge, have the various skirmishes that are unavoidable, until it comes to pass that, running ahead of some twelve or fifteen zombies one afternoon, I have to wrench the belt around, jerk sideways on Sidney, and, my son reaching for her the whole time, like he wants us to die here, I lob her behind us. Which is, I suppose, where my son's rear view is perhaps not as ideal as it usually is: he has to watch the lead zombie lower its mouth to the cat he named, suckle it dry. But there's nothing for it.

My legs are burning, my feet pounding, my front backpack lined with canned goods, and the sounds of our pursuers are more distant now, my son slack in his quiver like I've taught him, so as to preserve my balance. At least until a chance zombie, one of the fast ones, breaks from whatever it had been feeding on in a doorway. And of course Sidney was our last animal.

Now it's a race, the kind where I'm pawing, trying to be sure I really have saved one round in my left-hand pistol. The way I picture it is I'll find a corner up ahead, round it, slide to a stop, swing my son around and pull his forehead to mine, hold us together like that. If I do it right, if the slug's got enough powder behind it, I can end us both with one shot. And if not, he'll be first, anyway, and I'll be covered in him, and we'll have done everything we can do.

Except I'm wrong.

There is one more thing to do, as it turns out. One last line to cross.

While I'm looking for our corner, my son pulls his release strap, launches himself down in my backpack, his bad leg crunching under him, and, with his weight gone, I fall forward, skid on my palms, roll over just in time to see the new lead zombie almost to him.

"*No!*" I yell, reaching with my left hand, with the pistol, but my shot goes wild, and my son, he looks back to me then, and is so calm, so serene, so happy to be doing this for me that it would be a travesty for me not to stand, run, keep living. For him, always for him.

MY HERO

Vigilante Man woke with a start: someone needed him. He grinned and straightened his mask, pushed off from the foot of his bed to the open window, his cape sweeping behind him. Below, the lights of the city shimmered in the heat. A siren wailed, a dog howled, a movie-bound couple skirted the dark corner of a street only to walk into the headlights of a delivery van. You can't save them all. Vigilante Man had learned this long ago. You can't save them from themselves.

He leaned forward onto the sill, tilting his head for the voice that had called his name, trying to separate it from the gunshots and screeching tires and for a moment he heard it—a whimpering, a last breath, of someone cornered and alone, not knowing who else to call, what other name to say—but then a gloved hand muffled it. It had been coming from the bowery, though. Always the bowery.

Elastic Man's stomping ground.

It would be so easy to let him handle it.

But what if it was the Exacerbator again?

Vigilante Man shook his head no, please, and looked to the phone on his nightstand. All it would take would be one call to see if the hospital had been broken into again, or out of. If the

Exacerbator were free to wreak his special brand of havoc, bring the city to its knees. Last time had almost been too much, and the time before, and the time before. And Captain Impossible had even been around then.

Vigilante Man closed his eyes behind his mask, lowered his head. He was so tired. The closet behind him was filled with the carefully folded clothes of his alter-ego Evan Boanerges, ace accountant, and nights like these it would be so easy to slip into the white undershirt and faded boxers, wait for the alarm to wake him, then ride the bus to work. But then a paper would blow up against his trouser leg on the way into the office and he'd see the crime, the decay, the rampant destruction, and he'd look to the sky like everyone else. And what if that was Sherry down there anyway, backed into a corner of the bowery not even Elastic Man could squeeze into?

Vigilante Man clutched his cape—kevlar, because not all superheroes are bulletproof—and raised one leg to the sill then thought better of it, took Evan Boanerges' keys instead, locking the apartment door behind him, riding the elevator down with an old woman holding her dog. The dog growled at him. He stared straight forward at the row of buttons.

There was no theme music as Evan Boanerges entered the office the next morning, the pocket of his shirt lined with pencils like he was an engineer. It was part of the disguise.

His cubicle was third from the left, by the window. The special compartment of his briefcase held this month's issue of *Rescue Beaver*, the comic he liked to quietly make fun of during the lull before lunch when he made himself take a break from his projects, so he wouldn't get too far ahead of his coworkers. He didn't want to make them look bad. It wasn't their fault they needed calculators and deodorant.

In the false bottom of the drawer devoted to the last five years' tax codes was a back-up mask, just in case. His old one, with the elastic strap that always took a wad of hair with it.

At nine o'clock Boy Plunder showed up, the new temp. He had hidden pockets all over his body, shaped like staplers and hole-punches and tape dispensers. Evan Boanerges stared at him and Boy Plunder stared back. If he only knew.

Evan Boanerges crunched numbers for an hour, and then hunched over *Rescue Beaver* before it was really time: Sherry wasn't here yet, and she hadn't called in. Evan flipped through the pages humorlessly, Rescue Beaver's trademark taunts and obligatory tail-slaps suddenly banal and crude, his mask a mockery of heroism.

In the break room all the talk was about Morton in Special Accounts. Vanessa from Human Resources had seen his last health insurance claim, and he had some syndrome: Ehlers-Danlos. She said it with a question mark and a whisper and then looked to Evan. Evan pretended to be carefully preparing his coffee, though. The glass door at the front of the Hawkins & Daniels suite opened but it still wasn't Sherry.

Where was she?

Three cubicles over, Boy Plunder pocketed an electric pencil sharpener, his back to the office, his reflection caught in the observation window which looked out onto the whole city. The window was why Evan had turned down other jobs, better offers. Up here he was a guardian.

He held his steaming coffee to his lips and turned his back on Vanessa, but then Mr. Sharpes' wide frame filled the door and everybody's backs straightened.

His eyes were gleaming with managerial fury, the fist of his right hand clenching and unclenching.

Evan avoided eye contact, because, even in this suit, with

this bearing, this posture, still, there was something of the carriage of Vigilante Man there. Of rights to be wronged; of duty. Everything he stood for, Mr. Sharpes stood against, and for a moment Evan saw in his boss—from the knees down, at least—a similarly hidden identity, and then followed the three piece up to the leering grin, the bald head. Mr. Sharpes ran his hand through the hair he didn't have, told Vanessa to continue, not to stop on his account.

Vanessa swallowed and explained: Ehlers-Danlos syndrome simply meant you had too much collagen in your skin and bones. In extreme cases it could make a person rubbery. People with Ehlers-Danlos syndrome didn't *break* their bones, they *bent* them.

Evan winced, grimaced, grinned displeasure. He had known about Morton Collander's secret identity for months already. It was obvious: what kind of a name was Collander, anyway? But he was young, unlearned. Still slugging it out in the bowery every night, like one hero could ever make a difference there. Evan envied him his youth, though. How he always bounced back.

"It's nothing," he assured Vanessa, his coffee sloshing over the foam lip of his cup, onto his fingers. He pretended it hurt so they wouldn't suspect him as well. So they wouldn't find anything suspicious in *his* file.

Mr. Sharpes laughed.

It was his first time back in the office since his vacation. He had a tan six weeks deep.

"Saw your girl last night," he said, shifting the attention to Evan.

"My . . . my *girl*?" Evan asked, no eye contact.

Mr. Sharpes grinned: he was back all right. Stronger than ever.

"You know the one," he said, tracing her shape in the air like he'd actually *felt* it, "Sherry. The venerable Ms. Tombs."

Evan's cup exploded all over the front of his white shirt, and Vanessa laughed, and her friend laughed, and Mr. Sharpes shook his head and walked around the mess to the refrigerator.

For the days when Captain Impossible had been on patrol.

When Evan returned to his cubicle Boy Plunder was up to his armpits in a drawer.

"Lose something?" Evan asked, a Rescue Beaver line.

Boy Plunder smiled, nodded to Evan's pants.

"Wet yourself, boss?" he said, and in the instant Evan looked down—something Vigilante Man never would have done, as his tights were stain resistant, designed to wick even the slightest hint of moisture away—in the instant Evan looked down, Boy Plunder lowered his face to his waiting hand.

When he looked up he was wearing the old mask. The hair-pulling mask.

"No," Evan said, "don't, you can't, my secret ident—" but Boy Plunder was already up and over the side of the cubicle and running down the walkway throwing papers behind him.

Vigilante Man gave chase as Evan Boanerges, running only as fast as a non-heroic man could run in restrictive slacks and slick-soled shoes. He had to catch him, though. They flashed past the break room, the copy machine, and in the bend between the receptionist desk and the waiting room where no one had a clear view, Vigilante Man turned on the speed, sent Evan Boanerges airborne, so that he was able to hug his arms around Boy Plunder's thighs. They crashed to the tile floor together, sliding on the elbows of Evan Boanerges' suit to the front door and against it, even as it opened on the legs and feet and calves and person of Sherry Tombs. Her coffee was dripping from the hem of her skirt. She whimpered in a way Evan knew.

"You, you . . ." she said, Boy Plunder peering up at her through the eyes of the mask, and then held her clean hand over her lip, trying to stifle a laugh. "Evan," she managed to say at last, trying to help him up, Boy Plunder slipping out the door with contraband staplers and three-ring binders, "Evan, you saved me"—still not laughing—"again," and even though there were real tears in her eyes of some kind, Vigilante Man knew better.

It was simple: the Sherry that Evan knew had been replaced by a lookalike, a doppelganger, an automaton. The Exacerbator had wasted no time, as usual. What had he done with the real Sherry last night, though?

Vigilante Man peeled Evan Boanerges off and rolled himself on, snugging the cape on last. It was supposed to be fireproof, even capable of allowing him to glide short distances—say, from building to building—but flame-throwing hoods weren't quite as common as they were in *Rescue Beaver*—Evan snickered: *comic* books—and the need to move from building top to building top was only felt by the young, like Elastic Man and Kid Bonzai, the new college kid in Collections. And Boy Plunder, probably, depending on how weighed down with loot he was.

Vigilante Man sat on the foot of his bed again and thought about Sherry, the pivotal role she played in his life. How someday he would explain to her that he loved her not out of some misguided sense of protection—though the Exacerbator *did* make it seem that way—but because in the break room she always unscrewed the bottle from the lid instead of the lid from the bottle; because if she could get away with it, she'd wear control top hose under her bikini and then frolic in the surf, the water beading down her nylon legs. Because he needed someone to tell him to be careful and then send him out anyway and turn fast away from the window, already biting her index finger.

He would find her. He would stand at the window all night if he had to, but he would find her.

At three o'clock there was a knock at the door, and Vigilante Man crossed the living room of ace accountant Evan Boanerges, knocked back. The secret knock took a full minute and a half, but in the third series of the left hand diminutions the caller faltered, unsure—*Boy Plunder!*—and Vigilante Man slammed the door back to give chase.

The hall was empty but that meant nothing.

Vigilante Man reeled down the paisley carpet to the closing elevator and dived for it, his gloved hand forcing the twin doors open.

It was just the old woman again, with her dog. She pushed the down button and held it, waiting for him to stand.

Her and the dog both raised their lips at him.

"You shouldn't be out in your pajamas," she said around the tenth floor, and Evan closed his eyes and told her to just please shut up please, would she? and when the doors opened Vigilante Man was racing across the lobby, out into the night again, the doorman whispering a slight *go get em, big guy*, which is all any good hero really needs.

HOW BILLY HANSON DESTROYED THE PLANET EARTH, AND EVERYONE ON IT

He wouldn't say this later, because he'd be dead along with everyone else, blasted into a cloud of comparatively warm ash swirling around in what had been Earth's orbital plane, but it wasn't his fault. Really. Or, if there was any fault, it was that he was human in the first place, a species built specifically, it would seem, to push buttons clearly marked DON'T PUSH, a species that had only evolved in the first place because it kept reaching up to that next level of the beach instead of being satisfied with where it already was.

Given the chance, of course, Billy Hanson might have blamed the political situation of the lab he was with on a three-year grant, a political situation which was purely typical of any money-driven research setting, and beneath mentioning here except to say that there was the usual amount of pressure to collect some data, which could then be cribbed down into a prospectus for an article, dropped into whatever mailbox was marked for the latest pickup.

So, yes, had he had the luxury of time, Billy Hanson might have tried to shift the blame from himself, say it was the lab's fault, the same way he used to blame his older sister for grape juice he'd just spilled on the beige carpet, but, at the same time, had he *not* destroyed the Earth that fine June evening, then of course all the acclaim would have been his and his alone.

Because, almost on accident, he'd finally done it.

Not scheduled some prime observatory time—that had been scheduled for months, by some process Billy assumed involved darts—but decided, half on a whim, to let the computer cycle the telescope through one of its lighter diagnostic routines, which involved settling its crosshairs on some arbitrarily-chosen but rigorously-mapped set of coordinates, so it could fine tune itself, compensate for continental drift, smog, and all the rest of the usual variables, then hum and mutter to itself in binary for a while, finally give Billy the greenlight to redirect.

Which, to his credit, Billy Hanson almost did, thereby saving the Earth and everyone on it.

Except—and this is where the political situation of the lab he was working with comes into play—instead of automatically redirecting, Billy first did a manual check of the computer's date and time, as that was what was going to get stamped onto each image he was about to record. Last week, either as a joke or to maliciously corrupt everyone else's data (the latter, surely), some joker who'd pulled an early AM shift had set the date back enough years that the days and month-numbers still matched up, meaning nobody caught it for about thirty-six hours.

Luckily, nothing Billy had recorded that night was going into an article.

But that was just luck.

So, to be thorough—in a hostile environment, paranoia was just survival—Billy tabbed down to the clock, and, in doing so, happened to glance at the coordinates the telescope had already focused on.

It wasn't one of the naked-eye clusters.

Billy thought it was a joke, at first. Another joke.

It had to be.

But his face, it was so hot. And his heart, there in his chest. And he was even crying a little.

He had been right.

To back up a little: eight years ago, Billy Hanson had been halfway through his first post-doc gig, and, following the advice of his dissertation director, was already sketching out a series of questions which he could then narrow down into a legitimate research proposal. The key of it, his director said, was that he had to come up with something revolutionary, or at least revolutionary *sounding*. Because all those boards of directors, they wanted to be discovering the next big thing. Failing that, however, at least give them the promise of a valiant, newsworthy effort, with a data set that could possibly be recycled, even, so long as their foundation's name was still attached to it.

So Billy gave it to them.

His idea was that, if gravitational lensing was a real thing, allowing starlight to bend around bodies of significant-enough mass—and it was real, thank you—then shouldn't it also be possible to somehow focus through a 'web' or 'network' or 'crystalline arrangement' of stellar bodies, such that you were looking down the 'corridor' of their combined gravity, a sweet spot maybe just a few centimeters wide but infinitely deep, where the combined, equalized 'pull' would essentially be opening up a hole in space, maybe even time? What could you see then?

That was how he'd ended his proposal: *What could we see then?*

The headlines would be along the lines of "Mankind Looks for God," and have Billy's picture under it somewhere, smiling just mischievously enough to usher in another age, where the scientists could again be celebrities.

His project didn't even make the first cut, though, and no new age dawned, or took him for its darling, its media child. As his director said, Billy'd made the cardinal mistake: proposed a project which required no labwork, allowed no empirical results. Instead, all he needed was a pencil, some paper, and a brain. The *right* brain, granted, but still—the board didn't think their money would be best spent on a thought-experiment, one that could only ever be proven over the course of a million years, so, the next season, Billy and a colleague had a new, only slightly revolutionary proposal to submit, and he filed his Spatial Tunneling Debacle (as his director called it) into the bottom drawer, waited for the math to come.

Instead of the math, though, what Billy got that balmy night in June was proof, the kind that can be written to a digital image file.

And, because he was still in diagnostic mode, what he was seeing was beyond question, was untampered with, and, even better, whatever magical conduit of stars had lined up around his coordinates, to focus his series of lenses some exponential amount farther away than humans had ever even dreamed, they were each being recorded as well. So this would be a repeatable thing. If not physically, then at least in simulation. Let other people do the math, now; Billy Hanson already had the *pictures*.

It was all so overpowering that he didn't even bother to wipe the tear from his right cheek. He wasn't aware of it, really. Like a child, he was just smiling with wonder, leaning in as if to touch the screen.

On some as-yet unnamed planet an untold numbers of light-years away, a form of life wholly alien to him was sitting at what was probably a table, in what might be just another backyard.

As near as Billy could tell, this 'alien' was just staring straight ahead. For all Billy knew, though, this—this whatever-it-was, it was telepathically communing with its species, or gestating a litter of young, or turning to stone like it did every third year when the solar flares came, or using some of its complicated neck apparatus to filter the methane from its air, or whatever it breathed, if it even breathed.

It wasn't quite bipedal either, Billy didn't think, but did seem to be bilateral. From where Billy was looking, anyway.

Which is the exact point, not counting that first fish flopping up into the dirty sunlight, when humanity started to wink out of existence.

Billy Hanson's fingers fell to the keyboard as they had a hundred other nights, to adjust the second lens, which needed regrinding, really, not just another gear pulling on it, and his gravity peephole focused down across the universe, tight enough that, for an instant, the skin or covering of his subject's forelimb blurred, then snapped back in fine detail.

Billy nodded, backed off a hair—*had anybody ever done this, even? was he, in addition to testing the limits of physics, pioneering exobiology as well?*—and when the image finally settled again he nodded to himself, content, and only stopped when the alien cocked its head over the slightest bit, in a way that made Billy feel suddenly hollow inside.

This was the way the deer on the golf course he'd grown up by would stop, when they became aware of him and his sister, trying to sneak up.

"No," he mouthed, as if even voicing the word would give his position away, but it was too late.

The alien was tilting his head around now, then focusing up, back along the gravity tunnel, using some sixth or forty-first sense that Billy Hanson couldn't even conceive . . . had it felt the pressure of his stare? was this a species so hunted across both time and galaxies that it had developed a sensitivity to observation acute enough that it even kicked in across light years? Or— or could it even be knowledge-based, part of some maniacally epistemic religion, where knowing something about a fellow creature was tantamount to rape, or murder? It could even be that, sitting there, this alien was involved in the most dire offense known to its kind, so all its senses were already turned up, listening, feeling.

It didn't matter.

What did was that it had turned its head up to Billy Hanson in direct response to Billy leaning closer to his monitor. Nevermind that Billy was holding his breath now, shaking his head no, insisting that this wasn't in his research, that this shouldn't even be possible, according to the laws of physics as he understood them.

But neither should looking across the universe.

"No," he said again, instead of all the famous and enduring things he could have said. By then the alien was standing, looking back down the tunnel of stars, into Billy Hanson's heart, and it was only when the alien smiled that Billy realized what he was thinking: that this *was* a bilateral species, yes.

The only reason he noticed this was that the smile spreading across the alien's main face, it was lopsided, not really meant to indicate pleasure. The kind of smile Billy Hanson associated with an older cousin standing perfectly still in an empty hall during a game of hide and seek. Standing perfectly still and listening to the linen closet.

In that closet, Billy closed his eyes, tried to pretend he wasn't really there, and so never saw the backlash of power boring now through the fabric of space for Earth, to implode it with such suddenness that the brief vacuum left by it would, for a few breaths, pull all the surface flame from the sun, allowing what had been his solar system a moment of darkness, followed by a cold millennium marked by a shroud of dust, that, because the implosion had been so thorough, no longer contained even the building blocks of life, much less any memory of man.

That was all still seconds away, though.

A lifetime, an eternity.

In it, Billy Hanson opened his eyes, smiled the way you smile when you're caught, and, in the last and perhaps purest gesture humankind would be afforded, pulled the phone up to his ear and dialed the first six digits not of his girlfriend's number—he had no girlfriend—but of a girl from his department who always touched her right eyebrow when she laughed, as if there were a button there to make her stop embarrassing herself.

What Billy was going to tell her, maybe, was not to worry about it, you're beautiful and perfect and everything good, and I love you I love you I love you, please.

What he did instead was wait to call her for what turned out to be too long, and then, along with everybody else, wink out of existence with the phone to his ear, as if that mattered, what he meant to do.

LITTLE MONSTERS

We built the monster from leftover pieces of other monsters. A beak here, a tentacle there, claws all over. Gina kept pushing for bilateral symmetry, and I held my tongue for as long as I could—this wasn't her idea, after all—but finally had to say it over ordered-in boxes of noodles: that this is a nightmare creature we're foisting on the world, right? It's not *supposed* to conform to biology as we know it. That's specifically what's terrifying. Gina chopsticked another mouthful in, showing off that she could—of the two of us, I'm the barbarian—then shrugged and explained that bilateralism is particular to two things (chew, chew): whether or not the monster walks upright, might need to *balance* in some 'crazy, unmagical' way, and what gravity field it developed in. And of course it had to walk upright. Chase scenes are completely unexciting when the creature's just clumping and oozing and looming behind. Sometimes I hate her. But I wouldn't be doing this with anybody else, either. So, again, I told her sure, sure, this monster was going to be terrestrial, definitely, homegrown, and it was also going to get around without leaving a slime trail. And then I forked another bite in, let it swell until I had to close my eyes to swallow. The creature I'd been dreaming of for so long now,

I told myself, maybe I'd been hiding it half in the shadows of my mind on purpose, so I didn't have to get into stupid details like gravity. I guess what I wanted was the effect—people in the streets falling to their knees, screaming, the whole city stopping what it's doing, looking around to this new thing in its midst. Except, then, two days later, Gina stepped back, kind of rubbed her lips with the side of her hand, and said something was wrong. "What?" I asked, squinting in dread. "Peter," she said, cranking the garage door up to let us breathe, "so it, you know, it eats random citizens, pets, the occasional shrub or mailbox." I nodded. Hated it when she called me by my full name. It never tokened well for what was coming. This time was no exception: our monster needed some means of elimination. If not, then it would bulge, teeter, finally explode. And, if it was going to have that kind of apparatus, then we might as well assign it a sex, right? Unless of course we wanted to pioneer a third, fourth, or fifth gender—but we were already pushing it with the tentacles, wouldn't I say? I closed my eyes, could feel things collapsing inside me. We had to go to the kitchen to hash this out, and it took days, sketch after sketch. Not just the bathroom habits of monsters, but the mating practices. The dimorphism between the sexes—we were unimaginative, finally stuck with just the two we knew—and which sex was likely to be the most fierce, the most terrifying. The most successful. So the beaks had to go, turned out to just be vestigial, movie-inspired ornamentation. Driving to get more noodles that night, I hammered the steering wheel with the heel of my hand and cried, called myself *Peter* over and over. The next morning, then—I'd like to say after a night of furious lovemaking, but, well: more like acrimonious sitcom watching—we walked into the garage, found we'd forgot to disconnect the fibers from the switchboard. We salvaged what we could, our hands working in a unison we thought gone forever, but still, at the end of that terrible day, our monster was maybe a sixteenth of its former mass. The tentacles were still disconcerting, sure, but the claws were outsized now, had to go. "I'm sorry," Gina said into my chest, "it was me, it was me," but it had been both of us. I'm adult enough to know that, at least. So we did what we could with what we had. Again. Gina pulled back-to-back eighteen hours days just getting the eyes right—if it wasn't going to be fast, it at least needed to be able to spot its prey from a distance, have that kind of advantage— and I decided to save the tentacles (our last complete set) for next time around, and promised myself to harbor zero malice toward this monster, for not having been worthy of them. And then, finally, all of summer behind us now, it was done. Sure, we could tinker here, adjust that, shade this over a scratch, but the good artist knows when to put the brush down. And we could pretend to be good artists, anyway. "Well?" Gina said, her arm around my side, my arm draped down across her far shoulder— you love whoever you climb the mountain with, right?—and I nodded, hit the button in my hand, and the garage door creaked up behind us, bathing the slick cement floor in early morning sunlight, and, just like the two times before, our little monster hitched its backpack into the right place and we unleashed it on the world, out into the river of children leading to the playground, to kindergarten, each of them perfectly designed to wreak its own particular brand of havoc on the world, to never ever *ever* stop until the helicopters made it. And, if the city's breath caught in its throat a bit when our garage door came up, if it looked our way for maybe a moment longer than usual, then we never knew it. We were too busy watching her walk away ourselves.

THE HALF LIFE OF PARENTS

Zach had never given Muppets much thought, before meeting his in-laws.

All through his and Kayla's courtship (two years, four months), she'd managed to only mention her parents in passing, and, as they'd had the justice of the peace marry them shortly after a certain pregnancy test, and he had a thing about large groups of people and the not-so-great outdoors anyway, meeting her parents at the wedding hadn't been an issue.

Really, everything Zach knew about Kayla's family could be boiled down to one school photo: her brother, forever six years old, never going to learn to swim.

The age he was when he died, *he* probably would have been into Muppets, Zach said to himself, standing in the bright doorway of his in-laws' musty home.

Her dead little brother would probably think this was the best thing ever.

Not Zach. Not so much.

And Kayla could have prepared him better, he thought. There'd been a whole four-hour, last-minute road trip where she could have mentioned Kermit in passing. Just to soften this blow.

She was still holding his hand, though. That was something.

Maybe it was weird for her too, after all these years gone. All these years pretending her parents didn't exist.

Thirty minutes from getting here, her voice reverting to a sixth-grade squeak, she'd called them, surprise. Hi, Dad. Guess who's coming home? Guess who's almost there already? The idea was to lead with her shiny new husband, sneak the baby news in with an excited shrug, a few nervous bats of the eye.

A lifetime too soon, now, here they were, Zach's parent-meeting khakis wrinkled from the drive.

It probably didn't matter.

On the other side of the wood-paneled breakfast bar dividing the kitchen from the living room, was who had to be Kayla's mother, Marcy. She was poking her head over the bar. And her torso. Her crazy limp arms.

He could tell she was a she from the yarn hair, the overkill lipstick.

Kayla's father—Zach was suddenly at a loss for his name—was caught partway up the hall, just on the other side of the brick planter with the fake plants, the planter that would come up to about Zach's belt, were he over there.

But he wasn't going to be. He could already tell.

Kayla's father's eyes rattled to a rest in their shallow plastic lenses, exactly as if they were settling on Zach, and on Kayla, the new couple.

Zach smiled an uncomfortable smile, made one hundred-percent sure he still had that deathgrip on Kayla's hand.

"H-hello," he said, not sure if he should be looking directly at these Muppet parents or not—was that rude?—and over the rest of that first and only visit, Zach found himself unable to stop studying the phone on the end table.

It was old, flesh-colored, had the spiral cord and thick

buttons. A real antique. In his dorm freshman year, they'd all used these handsets as hammers, they were so strong, so heavy.

But that was the problem. That was the reason he couldn't look away from this phone.

Over and over, he kept trying to picture Kayla's dad darting out from behind the planter to catch the phone when she'd called, then somehow picking it up with his floppy arm. And directing it where? To which head?

"They never moved from their, their *perches* in the kitchen, and over in the hall, see," Zach told his first and only daughter Mira four years later, when she asked about legs.

Mira widened her eyes in a way that he could tell she was there all over again, looking at her grandparents with wonder, with awe. Like humans had descended from dolls, maybe, and Muppets were the missing link.

The story made Kayla cry. It was either because of the way he told it, where her parents were wild and unpredictable, fun-loving and whimsical, or because she was always on the edge of crying anyway, lately.

As far as Zach could tell, it was because of the ghost of Kayla's once-upon-a-time baby brother. She'd thought she was over him, until Mira started holding her eyes like his.

Instead of a splash pool in the back yard, Mira got washcloth baths.

Her food was all cut up into morsels so tiny that Mira had to use a spoon, never a fork. And still there was the chance of aspiration. But even Kayla could tell that, just as growing up with Muppets had left her with certain unshakable suspicions about the world, her following Mira around with an umbrella and disinfectant wipes wasn't all that different.

So she backed off, step by step.

To Zach, it was like the world was exploding in slow motion. He and Mira were on one postage stamp of an asteroid, and Kayla was on another.

For a while they could still see each other, but then Kayla went to visit her parents for a long weekend, to figure herself out.

Except it must not have worked.

A week passed, then two. Alone with his daughter, Zach found himself taking over all the worries Kayla had left behind. He'd always had concerns about the outdoors, but what was the indoors, if not just a trapped little piece of the park, the street, the alley?

Because Mira's little fingers could pry back the electric socket covers, he turned the power off at the fusebox.

Because anybody could knock on the door, he stopped answering it.

And every chance he got, he would fall to his knees and hug Mira, and tell her all the stories he knew, and paint Mommy as on a great adventure out in the scary world, fighting for him and for Mira.

It was his duty, he felt. And maybe it was even true.

Next to go were their shoes, because shoe laces can be a choking hazard.

They slid around in socks, and when Mira wasn't looking, Zach's breath would hitch in his chest at the weight of it all, and he would click the flashlight on, shine it at the ceiling like a beacon.

But that was a fire hazard. He had to be more careful.

Walking to just his voice in the hall a day or two later, Zach making sure his voice didn't shake like it wanted to, Mira's skating feet snagged a nail. It had pushed up through the aluminum strip separating the kitchen linoleum from the living room carpet.

She chirped surprise and fell forward, into Zach's arms.

They leaned back against the couch like falling into a trench in wartime. Zach smoothed her hair down, held her face against his chest, and only heard it when she did: the front door, jingling and jangling.

Zach's heart splashed into his stomach.

It was a break-in. He'd refused to deliver Mira to the world, so the world was coming for her.

He shook his head no, no, and then the front door opened for the first time in three weeks, turned into a square sheet of sunlight. It threw a hazy shadow on the wall Zach and Mira were staring at.

Zach felt a beat of recognition in his chest, like he'd been here before.

"What?" Mira whispered to him, and he crossed her lips with his index finger, so he could remember.

When nothing came, he breathed in deep, held Mira tight with his left arm and used his right to peel one of his socks off.

He bit the elastic top of the red-striped sock and ran his hand down all the way to the toe, then periscoped up over the back of the couch, his new, toothless mouth open as wide as his hand would go, in surprise.

Insert seven seconds of absolutely dead silence, here.

Until Mira's newly-socked hand (sparkly) came up beside his, looked around, opened its mouth in surprise as well.

"Mommy?" she said.

The shadow on the wall behind the couch took a step back, into the sunlight, her edges getting more definition.

"Kayla?" Zach said, the base of his jaw tingling.

The sharp intake of breath from the doorway told him everything.

"I brought, I brought—" she said, then said it better: "They want to meet their grand-daughter."

Beside her, then, two yarn-headed shadows appeared at her hips, their heads moving unnaturally fast, casing this living room.

Because her face was right next to his, Zach could feel the wonder spread across Mira's face.

"Close the door?" he said, over-enunciating so his hand could match up.

Or maybe the voice was actually coming from up there.

"Zach?" Kayla said, falling to her knees, "Mira?" and that was exactly when the phone on the shelf by the television rang once, long and perfect, the handset dancing in its cradle.

"I got it," Zach said, and, somehow, he did.

OLD MEAT

Dear Abby—

I've resolved not to inform the authorities on her, my wife. But I write to you to ask whether I should inform *her* or not, my wife. And, in trying to come to a decision, I of course ask myself if *I* would want to know.

In the daylight, the answer is rational, and simple, and obvious: yes.

But in the night, lying in bed with her, I'm not so bold. Yet at the same time I have to suspect I have nothing to fear, really. Have we not been married already thirty-eight years? Surely if she meant me harm, it would have happened well before now, yes?

And, though they're blameless in the sense that their intentions were innocent, still, some nights I curse our new pharmacy for even making me aware of my wife's condition. Better that I had just continued to sleep peacefully by her side, in my customary place instead of on the far side of the bed, away from the open window my wife has always insisted upon. Supposedly my repositioning to the other side of the bed was to lower my antihistamine dosage, and make me more alert. But I would take as many pills as necessary, Abby, not to have begun lying awake well past my usual hour, when the medicine had usually pushed me into sleep.

My initial thought that first night, of course, lying there without my glasses, everything in the house asleep save me, so that whatever happened might happen like a dream, was that my German Shepherd had crawled up into bed with me. But then of course I remember that Fetch, my German Shepherd, had been buried for nearly half a century.

I closed my eyes, looked again.

On her new side of the bed, my wife's profile was outlined by the sodium glow from the street lights.

She was sleeping as soundly as always, rasp in, rasp out, her chest rising and falling—unlike mine, I might add.

It's possible I had forgotten in that moment how to breathe.

Rising up from her pillow was the long, slender muzzle of a greyhound, or a particularly sleek wolf.

When I could, and I make no claims to bravery here, Abby, but when I could, I lightly said her name, and her breathing slowed instantly, almost before the whisper had passed my lips, and then her eyes rolled open, yellow and sickly and not hers at all, but— she's always been a deep sleeper, see. Though her eyes were open, she saw nothing. It wasn't her waking, but the animal.

I swallowed, and it was like thunder in my ears, and my knee as I repositioned it to roll out of bed clattered like sea shells in a muslin bag, so that, for the next twenty-eight minutes, I could only clutch what covers I still had and silently gulp air into my mouth, force it down my throat.

On the twenty-ninth minute, like a gift, her eyes closed again, resumed their darting beneath the lids, and the muzzle of which she wasn't even aware retreated back into her shadowed face with a thick, wet, and reluctant creak, and she coughed in her chest then rolled over all at once, flinging her arm across me so that the tips of her fingers rattled against my side for all the world like claws. But they weren't, Abby. They weren't.

She was my wife of thirty-eight years again, unaware of her transformation, and now I know this happens to her nearly every night, regardless of her mood, or the moon's. The animal in her, what it does as she sleeps is taste the night air from the open window in a way no man or woman ever could. And for now, anyway, that seems to be enough.

But will it always be, Abby?

Needless to say, she's of course caught me watching her in a different way since that night, watching her at the stove, or tidying the living room, or talking on the phone as if the world and all its particulars are in place, but the answer I give when she asks about my newfound interest in her—and I hope this is real, not just self-preservation—is that I think I'm falling love with her all over again.

At the same time, however, I know that some part of the scent she takes in at night is mine, is me.

So my question, Abby, it's not so much should I tell her—honestly, I don't have the heart—my question is that, at my age, can this still count as love? Is the outward appearance enough, never mind the hidden motive, which is simply my base desire to live?

Again, in the daylight, my answer to this is of course an enthusiastic yes.

In the night, however, my wife's snout rising from our pale green sheets, a purposeful growl emanating from her chest, my heart pounds in a different way altogether, one that has nothing to do with the sacrament of marriage. Specifically, it pounds in a way I fear is going to wake her.

Once the blood has stopped thrushing in my ears, though, and I can hear our fake eggs popping on the stove under her spatula, the question I have to ask myself is would *she* tell *me*? If, say, during my mid-day nap, which of late threatens to take the whole day, if *I* were becoming something else and knew nothing about it, would she tell me, or would she pull the covers up a nudge higher?

The latter, I think.

Instead of telling me, instead of making me know what I didn't need to know, she would count her blessings that I was such a sound sleeper, and perhaps this is what marriage really is, right? Not love *because*, but love in *spite*.

Or, in my case, *until*, I know.

Until she wakes.

But, too, I'm sixty-eight, Abby.

At this point it's a foregone conclusion that the end is near. I can feel it inside already, like a spill. The only unresolved portion of it is *how*. Meaning that . . . well, perhaps my wife's perfect teeth on my neck instead of a hospital monitor later, and a team of doctors leering over me, that might very well be the tenderest expression yet, the most intimate kiss possible.

All husbands and wives should love each other so, I think.

I count my blessings each morning, Abby, and pray quietly in the night, and leave this as a record, in case I've been wrong.

For now, however, I'll believe in love, and check my hands for cuts each night before bed—my skin is so thin, now—and cover any open wounds with two band-aids in the shape of a cross, so as not to excite her senses any more than my nearness already may be doing.

I mean, there's a difference in loving your wife and suicide, right?

Please share this with your readers, if you think it suitable. As for me, I'm off to nap now, in preparation of night, and in hope of morning, always.

—*'Old Meat,' Eugene, OR*

NEARER TO THEE

This is how it ends.

A concert in the park at the end of July, so the town can recycle some of its red white and blue decorations before the real heat of August arrives. Twenty years ago, the concert was the end of Founders' Day. It used to start with a parade at ten in the morning, followed with a barbecue and street games. But now the town's growing old and it's just the concert at dusk, a group of orchestral musicians culled from the classifieds of three cities less than a day's drive away, so there'll be no hotel expenses involved. It's their first time to play together. They're all supposed to have experience, though. Millicent from the events committee vetted them, guarantees they're quality, and a bargain to boot.

As for the town, the three cities half a day away, even, they're all as deep inland as possible, the heart of the heart of the country, as it were.

As for Dex, dragged to the park by his mother, he's thirty-four, on the rebound from his second real shot at life on his own. His long-term plans before he got evicted, cited, and finally arrested had been to make a circuit of all the trivia-based game shows, dominate them, and then sign endorsement deals for board games, return for the occasional championship tournament. It's a plan he came up with when he was fourteen, and it was more than enough to carry him through high school, to make him a local celebrity—he even won at bingo once, to everyone's consternation—but lately, pushing his mother's basket for her at the grocery store, nodding at the cartoon cereal he still prefers when possible, his mother's friends purse their lips at his presence; *their* sons, while not lawyers or doctors, are nevertheless stable, and already providing grandchildren.

Dex smiles, seeing all the old biddies on their blankets at the park, now. What he could do, he knows, is ask after his old classmates, as if he just wants to get a drink, catch up, relive a few old times. But it wouldn't be because he wanted to see any of them, really. It would be to watch their mothers' faces as they tried to come up with excuses to keep Dex from possibly infecting their children with his failure. His—though nobody knows this but him—*apparent* failure. His temporary setback.

What Dex has learned, though, learned the hard way, is that in game show contestant pools, the sole criterion isn't a well-indexed store of facts. No, you also need, at least in Dex's case, perhaps some legitimate grey in your hair. Otherwise the studio audience will suspect that you're a plant, a shill, working for the production company, keeping the winnings in-house. Nobody only thirty-four could have access to *that* wealth of data, could they? That wit.

But it's happening already now, the grey.

Just from being back in this town, Dex thinks. Another week here and he'll be a senior citizen too.

Until the next audition season, though, it's here or nowhere, he knows.

And, while he's here, may as well take in the sights, right? Re-experience the social milieu, for whatever it's worth. Remind himself why he needs to catalogue more facts, and more on top of that.

And who knows, there may even be some trivia squirreled away in the least likely place. Old people know stuff, after all, even if they don't know they know it. When did automobile windshields go from two-pane to single? What side of the presidential nominees do potential first ladies tend to stand on? How much currency is supposed to be in circulation in any ten-year period?

Not that Dex doesn't already have all this on tap, but talking about it with people who have been there will dredge up related facts—the trivia not written down in books. In addition, their withered faces will, if they humor him enough, serve as his mnemonic device. Never mind that it'll show them he's still got it. Show his mother, at least, so maybe she won't have to bring up the awkward issue of rent again over dinner.

This make-do orchestra, however—Dex has been listening to them tune their instruments and make introductions among themselves, run their hands over their pomaded hair and study the sky.

He's not expecting much.

Most of them, he's pretty sure, are younger than him, even. In this crowd, that means they're absolute children, and probably don't even have a glimmer of the history of whatever old standards the events committee's foisted on them this year. The polkas, the anthems, the Sousa.

For all intents and purposes, they may as well be a player piano, each of them a single pneumatic striker, activated by a notched roll.

Player piano. First exhibited 1876 by John McTammanny, though brought into production two years later by the Aeolian company. The source of many and grievous anachronisms in the bar scenes of scores of westerns.

Dex smiles, hides it with his hand like he's learned to do.

"Dexter?" his mother says, pulling his arm down, because he shouldn't hide his pretty face like that.

"Nothing, Mom," Dex says, and peels his eyes away from the stage, scans the crowd a bit.

Founders' Day, he wants to ask each of them. *Can you name any of the founders? The year, even?* Yet they each attend, with their blankets and their strollers and their buckets of food. Their troughs.

Again, Dex has to hide his mouth.

Best to sit down, appear docile. Not inflict himself on their evening.

He doesn't want to start paying rent, after all.

Still two months until the new season starts culling contestants. Two more months of this.

"Dear?" Dex's mother says, as if from far away, and Dex tunes in to the plastic cup of wine she's offering across the quilted expanse of their blanket. It's her new thing, treating him like an adult.

Dex takes the cup, salutes her, and chokes a swallow of it down, sets the cup on the grass by the blanket, where it can spill if it needs to. Alcohol dulls the mind. Dex might miss something, never know he missed it.

"Do you remember the time—?" his mother starts in, and the story she goes on with is about Dex being at this same concert at nine, or eleven, or twelve, or all of the other years. It was always the only time of the year that the trophies given out—for throwing cow chips, for catching eggs, for eating jalapeños, for spitting pumpkin seeds—weren't given out to him. Growing up, the park was no academic arena, no student assembly.

"Yeah, yes already," Dex says, rubbing the spot above his eyebrow he knows he shouldn't, as it makes him look unsure of his next answer. To deflect, he holds that hand up to his mom, raises the night's program close to his face, as if there's not enough light to read. As if he's really studying this, can't be bothered with remembering when he was nine, thanks.

His mother keeps her face exactly the same—he doesn't have to look to know—and tilts the plane of her attention away, to the *marvelous* band, and whatever magic they're going to be introducing shortly.

Let the willing believe, Dex says to himself.

It sounds better in its native French.

Idioms of the world for four hundred, please.

The violinist pulls his bow across the strings, effectively cutting the evening in two: the time before the band was making noise and the time after. The sound straightens Dex's back, grinds his teeth together.

He snaps the program down, studies this violinist and his string accompaniment, and decides he might have cause to *really* read the program now, thank you.

'Violinist, J. Law.'

Johnny Law, ha.

You caught me, Sheriff. Red-handed, a term most likely originating in Scotland—*Macbeth*'s setting, yes? anyone?—and referring to murderers, blood still on their hands.

Dex doesn't even cover his mouth this time, just watches the band ascend to their seats, narrows his eyes as the expectant silence washes across the crowd.

At least their suits match, more or less.

Something to look into, actually—Founder's Day doesn't have be a total wash, anyway. Do orchestras tend to wear tuxedo variants, or suits? History of? Reason for?

Dex writes it all down in his head, nods with Johnny Law's shiny black shoe, already keeping time, like he can't help it.

And then, like every year: Millicent Brown.

"Healthy as a horse, that one," Dex's mother whispers, and Dex remembers: Mrs. Brown's survived three husbands and two bouts of cancer so far. A hero for the geriatric set. What they all aspire to.

Dex shakes his head in disgust.

Millicent. Its diminutive being . . . what? Mildred? No.

Another note to scratch down in his head.

Names no longer in circulation, shortened forms.

Unlikely, but you never know.

The microphone screeches in anticipation of Millicent Brown's voice, and she draws back, her hand to her throat, aghast, insulted by this technology. From the front row a twenty-something grandkid—beholden to the events committee in some way, presumably—rises to the occasion, steps up, grips the microphone to adjust the gain but jumps back. It's hot, electric, would have fried an old bat like Millicent.

Excuse me, Dex says inside: horse. An old *horse* like Millicent.

"Lucky," Dex's mother says, in her best thee-not-me voice.

Dex shrugs, the microphone's swapped, and—screw it: Dex takes another drink of his unspilled wine, feels his mother watching him, stares straight ahead instead of acknowledging her approval.

"Tonight, we're lucky to have the . . . the"—Millicent stumbles, reading from a slip of paper—"Winston Family Orchestra, formed just now, as I understand, and possibly breaking up after tonight's show as well. Lucky for us then. A historic performance to be sure."

Genial laughter from the crowd. Understanding laughter.

Dex has to close and open his eyes three deliberate times to swallow this. They're making fun of their own inability to secure a real group of musicians. Like they're all in on the joke, and think it's a funny joke, and not about themselves at all.

The band's even grinning, trying not to.

Dexter drinks down the rest of his wine, scans the program for how long this will last this time. It'll be a challenge, remembering the duration of each piece—provided they keep to the standard arrangement, of course, or in the neighborhood at least—working up a TRT, *total run-time, thank you, next.*

And it's then that Dex sees it, as if peripherally. Or, not even sees it so much as *hears* it: Law, Brown.

He huffs air out of his nose: impossible.

It can't be.

And then it comes to him, the diminutive of Millicent.

"Dexter?" his mother says, her fingertips to his forearm.

Dex shrugs her off, makes her wine splash onto the blanket.

Yes . . . yes. But it can't be. Can it?

Dex is smiling now like the final round.

Law, *J.* Law, *John* Law, often called 'Jock,' at least in the early part of the century. Ten years before . . . what? King Tut's Tomb? The Lincoln Memorial? *Ulysses, Nosferatu*, the last Barbary Lion? Bea Arthur, Kurt Vonnegut, Jr.?

Listed below him like providence, somebody Preston, a Wesley something or another, a Henry, a Ronald Marie—two names at once!—and even a Cornelius. And that's the final blow, as far as Dex is concerned: Cornelius.

"Mom," Dex says.

She hears it in his voice, stops pushing her now-red napkin into the blanket. Turns to him like he *is* nine years old again.

"They—they can't," Dex says then, flinging his hand to the stage, at the orchestra about to launch into the event committee's first song. "It would be—it would be . . ."

"Shhh, honey," Dex's mother says, patting his wrist now, "they're just children, now. Milly says they're actually quite good."

Milly, no.

But close.

This is really and truly and actually happening.

"Mom," he says, not so much whispering anymore at all, so that now people—neighbors, ex-teachers—are swiveling on their blankets, taking notice, "Mom, listen. These, this band, they're, the names, *look*."

She does, they all do, and then settle their bovine eyes back on Dex.

He looks at them with disbelief, the first chords of the initial song already happening all around them, *to* them.

"Nineteen twelve," Dex pleads, and his old math teacher shrugs, and now Dex's mom is actually pulling him by the wrist.

Dex rips his arm away this time, stands from the blankets, and the way his mother gasps he knows she doesn't want another episode. But this can't be allowed to pass unacknowledged, either. Dex simply cannot *not* say it, the final answer to tonight's blaring question: "*Titanic*."

Instead of gasps from everyone now, and perhaps applause, followed by fear, which they should be feeling, four of the nine people listening to Dex turn away, to the stage, to the song coming together.

No need to embarrass poor Charlotte any more than she already is. Dex knows that's what they're thinking.

"*No!*" he yells, his hands fists by his pockets. "Brown, *Molly* Brown, the unsinkable, get it? Jock Law, violinist, Teddy Ronald, pianist, Percy *Cornelius*, freaking cello! Don't you see it? What this means?"

"What this means?" Dex's mom says, her voice all about talking him down, not really a question at all.

Dex pushes his hands into his forehead, pulls his hair, closes his eyes, and is about to launch into his trademark hysterics—"It's happening again, can't you see?"—when Officer Dampier, who knows Dex from the old days, takes him by the hand and upper arm, guides him forcibly away from the night's entertainment, so that, when the Winston Family Orchestra eases into what should be their trademark song, if anybody knew *any*thing, all Dex can do from the backseat of the town's only police car is bang his head against the unbreakable glass, scream and beg for them not to play *that* song, any song but *that* one, please.

Don't they understand what they're doing, the fire they're playing with?

But it's not fire at all.

It's ice.

As the orchestra swells with song, a series of unlikely collisions out in what Dex would know is the Kupier belt begins. Just a gentle tap at first, a nudge, but the end result of those tumbling collisions will be the disruption of a comet—one of the true icebergs of space—the disruption of its elliptical path through the solar system, redirecting it for a fateful intersection with Earth, a date with history that only unsinkable Millicent Brown will be able to record, if only she can find a pen. If only there are any pens.

Dex shakes his head no, no, his eyes finally settling on one old man near the stage, arranging and rearranging his lawn chair, as if that makes all the difference here.

Popular sayings, two thousand, please.

This is how it begins.

JUMPERS

Case in point: Ron's clothes started coming off about a quarter of an hour before lunch. At first it was just the cuffs of his shirt snapping open, one side of his tie getting longer and longer, but by the time he got back from the sandwich shop on the first floor, pants were becoming an issue his belt couldn't deal with. On the way to his desk Myrna smirked at him and his unkempt-ness; they were currently having a contest about who could pretend they had the most money, and this wasn't helping him. Behind him she threw away a tray of expensive chocolates after picking out the one she liked.

At his desk Ron went though the formalities: giving the clients he called free advice, and doing so loudly and clearly, as if he didn't need ten percent off them. But then his watchband came loose in the middle of an over-generous hand-flourish and landed deep in the mayonnaise of his sandwich. He held his breath, listening for the telescoping of Myrna's pupils, but she was in stealth mode, suddenly standing over his inbox.

"Too bad . . ." she said, eyebrows up in a fake arch.

Ron licked his lips, curled his toes to keep his loafers on, and told her not really, he'd been needing a new watch for months. One without all those extra, expensive features. And he hadn't really been hungry in the first place, just didn't want everyone thinking he was an android or something.

Myrna nodded, told him that she appreciated that, his efforts to maintain social decorum. It was the small things that would count, in the end. "But really," she added confidentially, leaning close, looking from side to side of his face, "you don't need to worry, doll. You're not quite symmetrical enough to be machine-made."

In response, Ron's hair caught whatever his clothes had, and mussed all over to one side.

It wasn't a good day.

He spent the next two hours dialing his own number so Myrna wouldn't know he was giving advice to the dial tone. One time he thought he caught her leaning a little too far over in his chair, eyeing the chocolate in her trashcan, but as it turned out there was a pencil on the floor she was after.

"You got the ti—?" she asked him when their eyes met, then made a show of looking to his desk, the sandwich and the watch now balled together in the same paper. She smiled an apology, turned instead to the huge clock set into the wall: 3:10. Ron's custom-ordered watch had been in the mayonnaise now for longer than any manufacturer would recommend. He would finish paying for it in four months.

He nodded to Myrna that it was no problem, it was an easy mistake to make. And he was forgiving—could *afford* to be forgiving. Even if his pants were at his ankles, now his knees.

Ron pulled them back up while sitting down—no small feat— then snaked his emergency suspenders out of his top drawer, shouldered into them under cover of his wingback chair.

He had to get out of here, out of the office, just for a bit. Hit one of the vendors on the street, salvage something like lunch from the day. It owed him that. He wasn't an android, after all.

He said this to himself over and over as he walked mechanically across the office, Myrna asking if everything was all right, he looked pale, pekid. Moreso than usual, she meant with a smirk.

Ron opened his mouth to lie to her, try to match her excess for excess, but nothing came out. He was empty, or too full. His mouth no longer worked. He looked hard and imploring to Myrna—trying to surrender, beg for mercy—and Myrna stepped out of character for a moment, asked it again, this time with feeling: "You all right?"

Ron shook his head no, and then the elevator doors were embracing him, isolating him.

In the chrome reflection his fists were buried deep in his pockets, clutching fabric, his elbows held close to his side, feet and knees touching, resisting.

A woman on the third floor tried to get on but Ron shook his head no. Somewhere above him a pencil was falling into a trashcan, returning to its owner with a chocolate treat proudly speared.

It didn't matter.

Ron put his watch back on and it didn't smell good.

On the street the delicate among the masses allowed him room to smear past, and he took it. He didn't need their approval. All he needed was a vendor, please. As if in answer, at the end of the passageway the crowd afforded him, there appeared a vendor, leaning back to counterbalance his tray. He nodded yes to Ron, once, and Ron stumbled to him, leaving his shoes behind like footprints.

Something wasn't right, though: the holes in the vendor's tray which should be holding peanuts or popcorn or something salty were all hollow and black. Ron tracked up the stripes of the vendor's apron to his face.

"Two dollars," the vendor's mouth enunciated, and then he

arched his eyebrows to Ron, waiting for a response. It was a challenge.

Ron grubbed a five from his wallet, didn't understand.

The man clipped it onto one of the tray's straps and then folded out twin aluminum shoulder supports, eased into them. The kind you wear at an amusement park ride. Next he smiled, and his teeth were filmed in rich chocolate, sick chocolate. He handed Ron a club sheathed in dirty sheepskin; the handle-end was strung to the tray, and Ron nodded his head to the vendor that he got it, yes, he was getting it, and by now a hesitant crowd had gathered. The vendor leaned back further yet, in anticipation, and started cranking a handle with his right hand, and when the first mole popped up out of his hole Ron clubbed its rodent grin back down where it belonged, and then another shot up near the back corner of the tray, smirking, and Ron clubbed it down as well, and then they were coming up two at a time, in impossible combinations, and the crowd was smiling behind their hands.

When his five dollars was spent, Ron offered twenty-two more, all he had on him. If only Myrna could see this, the way the tendons in the vendor's neck were standing out, the capillaries bursting in his eyes, the chocolate welling up in the back of his throat. Ron was a machine. Twenty-two dollars later he wouldn't surrender his club, either, but stood there, pants at ankle-level, shirt flapping, the crowd holding its breath for him, and that was approximately when I first came into contact with him, intuited the day that must have gotten him here.

After a series of long, mole-less minutes, Ron trying to will the vendor to turn that handle just one more time, he finally sheathed the club, looked left, right, and down, at his bare feet, and became small again. We've all been there. As he walked away, the crowd both giving him generous room and

49

pretending he didn't exist, I followed at a discreet distance, as the manual instructs, until—on the third time around his building—Ron looked to his watch for the time, only the time wasn't there. Under the beveled glass face there was just oil and vinegar suspended in egg yolk. He swallowed loud, stomaching some feeling, some realization, and then overcorrected for his mistake, his forgetfulness, and looked up the side of the building. All the way to the top, to the fire door on the roof the smokers had rigged. And he stared. And he had ideas that brought an easy grin to the corner of his mouth, and that was when I stepped forward, put my right hand on his left shoulder, locked eyes with him, and simply shook my head no. Not that. Not today.

He stared back at me, and, gradually—as they all do—the muscles in his face untensed, and he agreed with me for no other reason than that I had been trained to affect a caring look, been taught about the way the lips are and aren't held, the proper distance between eye and brow, how the tilt of the head can make all the difference.

Not today.

I stood there for a moment longer and then backed into the suits flowing by, became part of them again, my part of Ron's life over before it really even began. And this was only a Tuesday. Sometimes on a Friday I'll save six of them before lunch.

THE SEA OF INTRANQUILITY

This was back when we still hadn't figured out the key to living forever, back when all the dumb schmucks about to check out down on Earth would pay to have their minds warehoused in the chitinous skin of those giant low-grav shrimp and lobsters they'd let loose on the moon, in all the new oceans that happened when the craters filled up with industrial rain.

Back in the stupid days, I mean.

I was right in the thick of it.

See this scar, right here?

It's from then. Not from a giant claw or some antennae whipping back and forth like you'd think, either.

It's from a dame.

And before you jump on my case for calling her that, dial back to then if you can. Everybody was financing family crests, becoming instantly royalty. Dukes, princesses, counts, a few kings, an emperor or two, and 'dame,' that shuffles in there somewhere, I'm not just real sure where. Maybe it's like a knight?

Guys who've been reduced to p.i. work late in life, well. There weren't a lot of princes among us, I guess you could say. Mostly mongrels, if you want the truth, and even in that pack, I wasn't top dog.

My office was the storage room above a bar. When I could make it upstairs at closing time, it was also my bedroom. When I couldn't make it down, it was my cell. You get the picture. These weren't exactly my gravy days.

But then your mom walked in.

She carried her breasts before her like a platter of cookies, I swear. Just looking up and seeing her, I was ten years old again. But growing fast.

As for how she found me, your guess is as good as mine. I'd guess she lucked onto me in the Directory. For all I know, one of those gadgets she had lacquered into her fingernails could find a midpoint between Discretion and Gullibility, then associate a name with it.

Rock Turner, p.i.

At your service, ma'am.

I'd say your mom was all legs, except for her breasts.

It's been a clean two years since that day, but I'm guessing that if she walked through this door, I'd forget what I was saying all over again.

Just like then.

I was on the phone with a former client, trying to leverage another payment, even considering taking payments *toward* that payment, but when your mom sat down on the other side of my desk, I hung up as gently as I could.

"What can I do you for?" I asked.

She settled into this tall chair I had back then, crossed her legs like she'd just flunked out of leg-crossing school. At least the one for ladies.

I would have lit her cigarette for her, except for the bans. Everybody was afraid of lighting the atmosphere on fire again. What they were really afraid of was that smokers would be the only ones able to breathe fire, the only ones to come out the other side, but still, you could get fined, and, since they'd taxed smokes to hell and back, I'd quit carrying my lighter.

Until now, though, until I needed a good reason to lean forward, change my point of view, I hadn't much regretted it.

"My husband," she said. Because it had been highlighted in her script, probably. Because she'd seen all the old watchies, knew what was expected of her here.

I didn't care. Not that she was lying to me, and not that she was married. Really, the first, the deceit and how easy it seemed to come to her, it was what was making the marriage not so important at the moment.

Anyway, I won't bore you with the rest of what she'd made up to bait me in. It was the usual sob-story of being cheated on, a prisoner in her own house, victim of the fairy tale, all that. She even worked her own mom in somewhere, but then, towards the end, we got to the important part: her husband had checked out.

She didn't want to find him because she loved him, but because the house detectives were closing in on her, she was pretty sure.

You might not remember that, though, right? 'Check out?' It wasn't the technical term, was just what you said about somebody when they'd called the Service. Had one of their bots come out, attach that thing to your head. The SoulSucker.

Everybody remembers them.

Ten minutes with a SoulSucker and the most important parts of you were in storage thee hundred K away, had become a kind of transparent amoeba or bacteria in a giant lobster's shell. You were part of its armor, now. You were in storage.

As for the tech on that, I'm probably the wrong detective to ask. Far as I could follow, with crustaceans, we'd always thought they were native to Earth. Cockroaches of the sea, all that. Good for dinner and date, just creepy the rest of the time. But, turned out, they were creepier than we'd ever thought. They weren't from Earth at all, had just drifted down some millions of years ago. And, the only reason they were all small and puny, it was our sludgy gravity, shaping them. Keeping them down.

I mean, yeah, on the moon they still had that buggy look, don't get me wrong. But they were *monster*-huge, and their proportions were just different enough to make you nervous, and, lo and behold, get enough of them in the same heavy-water tank like you've got on the moon, and bam, them suckers can lock together like puzzles. Not to make some even bigger lobster or shrimp, but . . . nobody really knew. Some natural part of their life cycle, or were they huddling up to plot against us?

You could take a sub, pry them apart, but they'd just fall away dead, and those ones that fell away, none of the other lobsters or crabs would eat them. It was like they were poisoned, or fallen soldiers.

Like I said: creepy as hell.

Still, we're pretty smart monkeys down here on Earth some-times. We tested the water and, surprise, when they all locked arms like that, got their mental space orgy on, it released some-thing into the water that changed the other lobsters that were still solo, waiting their turn.

It changed them so we could use them like storage devices.

And that's where your dad was, evidently.

In one of a hundred and twenty-two giant lobsters in uncharted lakes on the moon.

The rub, though, it was that somebody had put him there.

He hadn't made the call himself.

Somebody'd dropped a serious dime on him. My job was to roll it off.

* * *

The blast to get me lunarside was the usual thing.

I softened it with four hours at the bar—two on Earth, two on the moon, all the drinks there swirling with calcium so that you'd have grit in your mouth after tying one on proper.

Like I care about a little chalkmouth.

I wiped my lips and found myself a captain. Not the one your mom had hired, because I do have a few self-preservation instincts, mind.

The guy I found was a girl. She carried a laser bullwhip on each hip. I didn't ask what for.

Hand in hand like she'd claimed me for the night, we made our way out to her ship and she took us across to the Sea of Tranquility.

All the seas kept the same names they'd had when they were just craters. Like I say, these were the stupid times.

As for why we knew to go there and not to any of the others, it was that the investigation into your mom, it was only three days old, meaning your dad couldn't have checked out more than four days ago. So—I didn't get my license for nothing—of course he'd still be in the Sea of Tranquility. It was the staging area, was where the sensors monitored whether your personality was going to synch up with your shrimp or not.

If not, no big deal, they could move you to a crab, and if that wasn't love at first insertion, then they'd just load you onto one of the krill. On Earth, they were a joke, were nothing, but in low-grav, they were zeppelins, floating through the new seas. They were gods, dwarfing any of the lobsters or crabs. Who knew, right?

Anyway, the first week out of your body, they liked to keep tabs, just to report back to the family on Earth: "Papa Walter's loving it up here! He's in the third right-side leg of a snow crab forty feet tall! He'll be ready for whenever you decide to download him!"

You know the racket.

To this day, no one's ever been properly downloaded.

Evidently that same chemical or whatever the lobster huddles infect the water up there with, it's like mind-glue for any consciousness that comes into contact with a crustacean and then stays there long enough for the eggheads to solve death.

Mated for life, yeah?

I don't need to tell you.

Anyway, this is where I get to say it: The Sea was angry, and so was I.

Nice, yeah?

It's no joke, either. The trick with water on the moon, it's that just barely lowering your ship into the water, that creates a wave, right? No big deal on Earth. On the moon it's not either. At first.

Those round craters, though, something about their specific curve, they magnify the ripple, pass it back and forth a few times in low-grav, so that, next time you see it, it's a swell, kind of rocks you back and forth, makes you reach for the rail.

They didn't let these craters fill all the way up, though. They didn't want the monster lobsters crawling from lake to lake. Hard to track that way.

So, these swells, they just crash into what for them's a wall, then come back harder, and harder, until, about eight minutes after you set down, you're staring down a tidal wave. One with giant red antenna whipping back and forth in it.

Your mom, she wasn't paying me near enough.

The captain I'd hired, Lorenga, she'd tapped into the Service's monitors, of course, knew which lobster had the most recent rider, but we were only just figuring out what depth it was when I looked up into a wall of water balancing above us like in a Japanese painting, where the falling edge of the water's all curled in and dripping foam.

Lorenga felt my silence, turned around.

Or—okay, not exactly silence. But I wasn't screaming either. This is back when I still carried one of those dicta-wills, that you could talk into, change on the fly.

I was willing my remains to your mom. Just so she'd have to pony up for transport, sterilization, interment.

It would about equal my bill, I figured. And, it wouldn't be going to me, but she'd be paying it anyway.

I've tried being not petty. It's not all it's cracked up to be.

But then, that wave already changing the temperature of the thin, manufactured air around us, Lorenga slid her two whips off, lit them with a harsh crack.

I didn't even have time to step back to the wheelhouse.

She slashed forward, using them in sequence, and cut us a hole through that wave.

The ship rose under us, but she'd cut tall enough that we barely had to duck.

Afterwards, I was laughing.

She looked to me just long for me to see the complete lack of humor in her eyes, just long enough for me to wonder if she had been manufactured, if she still had to charge up at night.

And then a thick red feeler wrapped around my waist, pulled me into the water.

Your dad's lobster?

It had found us.

Because I hadn't thought ahead to get fitted with gills—I could have billed your mom for it, even—I had to try thrashing and screaming and drowning, finally biting into that meaty feeler.

It didn't care even a little.

We were diving, diving.

Above me I was pretty sure I could see Lorenga's twin whips, but then a snow crab ghosted in above the lobster, its spidery legs so graceful that, right before I passed out, I think I probably smiled.

Above us, I'm sure the surface of the water was calming back down.

I came to with my head stuffed up into an air-filled divot that had been chipped into some underhang in the crater.

It was barely big enough for my head.

I pushed down from it but all around me there was just water, all lit up that eerie way you get when the atmosphere's thin and unreliable.

I came up for air, gulped it down, got a lungful so I could look around some more.

A giant crab was scuttling down the wall to me. It had just surfaced. There were still bubbles of air roiling off its skin.

Working delicately with its hind legs, it delivered three of those bubbles up past my neck, into my headhole.

The air was warm and musty, and I loved it, breathed it all the way down to my toes.

When the crab left, I pushed down again, my hands keeping my place, and looked around.

All along this underhang were other people. Just bodies and legs. And arms.

This was the refrigerator. We were in storage, and not the good kind. We were what the krill had been on Earth. We were those little pieces of meat drifting down from the unfiltered sunlight. Perfect little pieces of meat.

I gulped, held, and looked below me.

The floor of the sea was crunchy with crustaceans. All crawling over each other, looking, from this distance, just normal-sized.

Way in the distance was a giant, impossible disk. One of the huddles I'd heard about.

What were they doing?

I wanted to laugh, I guess. I needed a drink.

I shoved my head back up into its new home, breathed deep.

So this was it, then.

Rock Turner flies to the moon, goes for a swim with the pretty bugs, doesn't come back up.

I imagined the headline: NEW SHOW ANNOUNCED! YOUR PARTICIPATION IS VITAL!

Nothing about me, yeah.

Like your mom was going to report me missing and dead?

I kicked just to try to stay warm. Watched that giant snow crab move past.

And then it came back to where it had been. Like it was running from something.

Lorenga.

She was underwater, had both whips going, some kind of powered flippers on her feet.

She cut the tip of one of the crab's legs off. The meat was flaky, white, perfect.

I coughed, almost breathed water, had to go up for another drink of air.

When I came back, found her, she was on the crab's head, one of her whips severing an eyestalk, her mouth open in rage, her last few bubbles screaming up and up.

At which point your dad entered the scene.

The thing about using space lobsters as storage devices for people's minds is that it wasn't an entirely known process. Then or now. I don't know why we ever thought it made sense.

My suspicion—this is now, not then—it's that the eggheads didn't really care about putting grandpa on ice until some later date. No, what they wanted to do was infiltrate those huddles. My guess is they were all holding their scientific breath, waiting for a storage lobster to join a huddle. At which point they'd harvest the person they'd put there, wake them up, see what was what.

Meaning maybe that mind-glue sticking people to their lobsters, it was a defense mechanism, yeah?

That's not my case, though.

Pay me to care, I'll try. Don't pay me, and—well, you'll see.

As far as storage went, anyway, putting somebody almost dead into the exoskeleton of a giant crustacean, that crustacean, it didn't really seem to mind. It was like having a barnacle or something, I guess. An itch in a place it could never quite scratch.

Try to stuff somebody in who's all the way alive, though, and, yeah, one of those barnacles, it's going to be more than an itch.

Instead of just hanging on, existing, your dad had fought to the top of his lobster, was at the reins now.

His giant lobster—he, *him*—cut up through the water like, I don't know. Like some monster born in the depths of the universe, some monster from when the stars were young, some monster that had cut across millions of light years for just this showdown.

With his big claws, he snipped off one of the snow crab's legs. Then another.

The snow crab reeled back, mute, offended, and Lorenga took its other eyestalk then dropped her whips, started doing that full body shudder of somebody who's finally got to drown.

Your dad pinched her delicately in his claw, kicked hard for the surface, and, even now, I would give whatever it took to have been on the shore right then. To see this giant claw burst through the water, a limp woman in its grip, a thousand dusty galaxies as backdrop.

Using his claws as no lobster ever had, then, he climbed the crater's wall, left Lorenga coughing on the rim of a cliff.

And then he came back for me.

Evidently—this is just from something one of the eggheads said, it's not like me and your dad talked or anything—evidently your mom's scent had still been on me. When I'd dipped into the water, it had shot all through the sea, had woke your dad up from his long sleep.

And he woke up mad, let me tell you.

He knew who'd put him there.

Not ten minutes later, he nipped my foot with his claw, pulled me down from my headshaped hole.

Instead of saving me like he had Lorenga, though, he pulled me into his maw of a mouth, swallowed me whole.

If you've never been inside a giant space lobster, well. I don't recommend it.

He climbed the crater wall again, stepped around Lorenga— I've never seen Lorenga again—perched on the cliff's edge. Then he used what he'd found in the lobster's backbrain: potential. Old programming.

From the side, I'm guessing his giant lobster body must have looked like a dragonfly. At least when those massive, delicate wings unfolded from his shell, flapped to get dry.

We lifted up, up, batting hard against the thin air—inside the stomach was dry, which made no sense to me—and then made history.

Instead of taking a transport or a tube back to Earth, your dad flew us there under his own power.

My eardrums burst from the pressure and I clawed at my ankles deep enough to bleed, but I was awake the whole time. And screaming.

That's not where this scar comes from, though.

That'd be your mom's handiwork.

After we cut through Earth's puny defenses—they were all for ships and transports, not for flying lobsters with laser eyes and killer claws—we burned through the atmosphere, your father's wings turning to ash with us five miles up.

We made a crater when we landed, and this crater, I crawled up from it all by myself, had no clue that, on the moon, the krill had risen to witness your dad lighting off for the territories.

Right about the time we were crashing down, the monster crabs and lobsters and shrimp were piling onto their huddled brothers and sisters.

Until then, we thought the way they'd locked arms, one behind the next, it didn't matter much.

They were a disc, though.

The krill drifted into place below them, started glowing with power. They were the engine, apparently. The battery.

As one, twelve discs broke the surface of the lunar seas, their backs thick with giant space lobsters, with delicate interstellar crabs, and then they turned away from Earth. Never to come back.

People wept, reached to the sky for these creatures they'd never known to worship. The usual story.

Like I cared.

There were endorsement deals, talk shows, new digs for a while. My name was even on a toothbrush.

Everything dies, though.

Except me.

Evidently, the unregulated pressures inside a mentally-hijacked space lobster's stomach, especially when that space lobster's taking on its interstellar dragonfly form, they're unique and transformative, to say the least.

And then there was the chemical wash part of that ride, and the exposure to cosmic rays, and whatever else nobody's been able to replicate, especially since all our gods have abandoned us.

What did it all add up to?

I had died in transit. I was still dead. All my measurable life processes were flatlined, but it didn't matter. I walked up out of that crater on my own, smiled for the cameras, winked at this one cute little number in the front now.

And, when that parade was all over months later, I went to see the queen.

Your mom.

"You," she said, standing in the doorway, her voice sharp enough to draw blood.

I handed her my bill.

She laughed, wouldn't take it.

"I don't traffic with the dead," she said.

"People pay for this bite," I told her, snapping my teeth to show.

"And does it work?" she said.

I found somewhere else to look.

We figured out how to live forever, sure. Just be dead, but walking around.

Now that there are no more space lobsters left to hitch rides in, though—well. I'll be at your funeral. I'll be at all your funerals.

"You were supposed to bring him back alive, anyway," she said, her hand to the door like she had no time for this.

"Bring him back so you could kill him again?" I asked.

My skin by then was pretty decayed, I guess, so it was hard to get a good smirk going. But I tried.

It made your mom's hand reach up to her own face. For the wrinkles she'd pancaked over.

They're showing even more now, aren't they?

Good.

"You can't prove I put him up there," she said, smoking a cigarette she'd lit herself. The atmosphere somehow not turning to fire.

She passed the cigarette to me and I breathed deep, couldn't even begin to feel it charring my lungs.

"That he came back is proof," I said, blowing smoke. "If Earth's gravity hadn't found him again, he'd have snipped you in half."

"You don't like me very much, do you?" she said.

"You sent me to the moon to die," I told her, just like I'd rehearsed on the drive over. "Just to tell the house detectives you'd given it an honest effort. You'd even have a receipt to enter into evidence."

"I don't need a receipt anymore."

"I could tell them what you did."

"You'd trade your version of fame in for that? You'd just be a passenger then. A victim. It would be my husband's revenge that made you like you are. Not your own . . . what did you call it?"

"They were putting words in my mouth."

"We needed a hero."

"Needed," I said.

"Very past tense," she agreed, and then I felt that tap on my shoulder I always feel about this time in a case.

This time it was a pair of giant, vatgrown butlers.

The one on the left came at me with a hot katana.

It flashed out of nowhere, split me from my cheek, here, down to my armpit—is the feed picking this up?

Here, I'll lean in.

Yeah, pretty ragged.

Turns out when you're dead, though, they can just sew you right back together.

Anyway, in case I go infectious at some point, can make everybody else live forever just like me, the Service keeps agents in the bar, now. So I won't go getting cut in half anymore.

That doesn't mean I've forgot, though.

That first time your mom strutted in? I was on the phone, collecting a payment.

That's what this recording is about.

If I did it live, I'm sure they'd find a way to stop me. And, I would be leaving this on your mom's machine, but she won't accept my calls anymore.

With me, though, you always pay. One way or another.

Here, let me . . . recognize this?

Yeah, you do.

Cute little crawfish. Been keeping it in a tank under my desk all this time.

Oh—I mean *him*, not 'it.'

When I crawled up from that crater your dad made falling from the heavens, I'd crawled up alone, yeah. But now *I* had a rider. In my pocket.

Gravity had found your father again, just like I told everybody.

In low-grav, with the stars as backdrop, he was a monster, a giant, a space god.

Here on Earth, well. As you can see.

Was that a rocket in my pocket or was I just glad to see your mom again?

The first.

Take a transport up, open the airlock, let Daddy here float out, and, bam, instant spaceship. Immortality. Eternity awaits. Live forever, *ma*dame.

Or don't.

Funny thing about this is, I don't even really need to eat anymore, right?

But—here goes, here goes, into the hangar—I can still chew, as you can see.

Legs and all, baby.

Nice, good. Tastes like hope. No, no. Tastes like *justice*.

So, if you need my services again, you can find me in the Directory, I expect. I'll be filed under Dead, probably.

Dead and Loving It.

Bye, now.

THIS IS NOT WHAT I MEANT

What Paula tells us at the Saturday morning sales meeting is that we won't know who it is, this inspector from Corporate, a place so remote from our little corner of things that it might as well be another world. And then, after saying that, she leaves a silence we all know how to interpret.

For her last round of training, she spent three weeks at Corporate, and so may just recognize this inspector, this interloper, this—Corporate's word—'visitor.'

"And I'll be on the floor myself, of course," she adds, managing somehow to look each one of us in the eye.

Maybe it's a trick she learned while she was away, or maybe it's a natural ability all the women in her family have. Either way, when she doesn't smile, I feel compelled to grin, like I'm making up for her seriousness, just trying to maintain some balance here, keep us from tipping all the way over into the absurd.

Of course my efforts go unappreciated, but, too, it's not like that's in my job description either. All I'm supposed to do is man my counter, wipe away the smudges, show the customers the sunglasses they want to see, and maybe the ones that cost ten dollars more too.

Before I know it, the week before the visit's smeared past, simply gone, and, like we're secret service agents, coiled white wires snaking up to our ears, we all know that the visitor is in the store. His presence crackles across all of us. Nobody whispers, but—it's like the whole store has suddenly taken on the whimsical consistency of a watercolor, and the visitor is wading through it, stepping down deeper into the floor than any of us can, leaving swirls and eddies and ripples down whatever aisle he chooses.

When Paula walks past my counter, her smile is so mechanical, has so little to do with her eyes, that I smile almost to the point of laughing, have to clamp my hands over my mouth. Then, standing like that, I see what Paula's doing: walking in advance of the visitor for us, telling us with her presence to be on our best behavior, that the moment is here. That he's coming. That we should be casual, like her. Natural. Ourselves.

For a long moment I have to close my eyes to compose myself.

When I look back to the store, the only place I can even remember anymore—did I ever have a mom, even, or did Paula just raise me in the stockroom?—I see the visitor for the first time. Like we've been told, he's not wearing a suit. Nothing that obvious. Like we've been warned about, though, he does have an otherworldly carriage, his head turning from Casuals to Intimates as if they're wholly new, each rack and rounder a complete and total surprise, a wonderful new artifact to catalogue.

From last Saturday's sales meeting, and from the handwritten notes Paula's been leafing into our reshelves, we know to smile and grin no matter what this visitor does. Because he's from the rarified atmosphere of Corporate, yes—we can't forget that— but, too, because there may be some new protocols in place this visit: perhaps he's been told that it's not enough to observe us in our routine. Maybe this time, he wants to see how we react under stress, in sales situations we haven't been specifically trained for.

The way Paula put it in the breakroom while I was eating my pimento cheese sandwich was that, if I'm asked to give the visitor, say, a chimpanzee, my response should be along the lines of 'With or without sign language training, sir?'

What this means is that, as the visitor approaches, my mouth is so full of answers and smiles and possibility that I'm afraid to do anything, really, am more than thankful when, for reasons only he knows, he stops with his hand on the shoulder of a clearanced pullover, a look on his face of total and absolute detachment. As if he's communing with Corporate, possibly, or channeling the board of directors somehow, through the lines and ridges in the palm of his hand.

But it's deeper, too. The way his lip trembles.

What—what's he thinking, remembering, reliving?

Have we marked that pullover down too much?

After checking to make sure I haven't put the same one on at some point in the day—it's happened, and more than once—I arrange the hangers under my register and stack all my receipts by length, and don't say anything.

Whoever acts the most 'retail normal'—Paula's term, grafted over, we presume, from 'business casual'—whoever pulls it off the best for the visit is supposed to get a twenty-five dollar gift certificate to the store.

Not that there's anything here I want anymore—have I really been here that long already?—but still, hidden under that brass ring is a spike: if whoever does the best job is rewarded, then what of that person who messes the whole visit up?

Paula is capable of anything, we suspect.

So what I do is smile, just not too wide, like I'm guilty. And keep my hands always touching something, so they won't visibly tremble. And, because of all that, maybe, because I'm projecting such a vision of control, of 'retail normal'—or because I'm an obvious weak, shrieking link—the visitor sidles up to my counter, looking up at me with just his eyes, as if already suspicious here. His fingertips hover over the glass just above my five rows of sunglasses, arranged first by brand and then by price.

He's just a customer.

"Something you remember from the island, maybe?" I hear myself say.

Above me, my security camera focuses down on the back of my neck. I can feel it like a spinal tap.

The *island?*

"How can you know about that?" the visitor whispers back, a hiss almost, looking at me sidelong now, as if about to walk away, pretend not to have heard.

I open my mouth to speak, to lie with all pleasantness, to explain how of course I know about that weekend when even his wife doesn't, but then—then I don't know where that comes from either: that he's married; that the island is a secret, a treasure he's buried so deep it's making him sick.

Maybe it's the way he hovered his fingertips over my glass. Yes. That has to be what it was. I've seen so many thousands of people place their fingers there that I can read their lives now from the way they splay their hands.

Because otherwise.

Otherwise I don't know how I could know.

And I don't anyway, or only ever did in order to say that one thing. Like he *needed* me to say it.

Only, now, there's nothing left. I can feel my mouth moving, and my face around it.

The visitor angles his head over, his eyes boring right into me now.

"Candace?" he says as much with his face as with his mouth.

Though it's not a thing I do or have ever done, as far as I can remember now anyway—which, granted, isn't that far at all—I touch my hair, look at it.

It's still brown, still me. But not, too.

I laugh, don't cry, thrust a pair of suddenly-red sunglasses across the counter at him.

When he puts them on, as if that, really, is the only thing to do with them, as if I've left him no choice in the matter, I see that the red-tinted lenses are bubbled, that this is the demo-pair we use to sell the leather, heat-resistant cases.

Before me now, blind to all this, maybe literally blind with those glasses on, the visitor has his head tilted back, is studying all parts of the ceiling at once.

"How much?" he says.

"Eighteen months or two quail eggs," I say, like it's a thing I say every day. Like that pair's even for sale.

"Not the—not the whole quail?" he says back, his fingers to the glass in some configuration so dense and elegant I almost lose my breath: what I can see is sand, matching up with other sand, and children's feet, a freckled girl even he's forgotten by now, except insofar as Candace is, to him, her, grown-up.

What the freckled girl and the visitor found in the sand that day was . . . I don't know. Something to do with a bird, maybe? That he thought of the whole ride home, and then never again?

Am I really going to cry now?

"You'd have to talk to financing about that," I tell him, nodding across the store to Customer Service, trying to tell him with my eyes that *that's* where he really wants to go here.

He looks with me, nods. Doesn't see the tears running hot down the back of my throat. What I'm wishing with every fiber of my being is that I was Candace, whoever Candace is, my hair sun-bleached and impossible, perfect, my cheeks dusted with freckles I secretly don't regret. That I was anybody but me.

What the visitor does after looking across the store to fix Financing in his plans is touch the rack of cheap sunglasses, their arms oily from being tried on so much. He touches it and it starts spinning, only, instead of just going around, it goes up and down *and* around. Like a carousel.

He smiles about this, spins it again, finally starts nodding, looking over the top of his glasses at the store.

". . . this—this is all a dream, isn't it?" he says, "like last week, right?"

"I—I don't . . . it's supposed to do that," I tell him, my eyebrows showing my worry, I know. "Paula—Paula says if they'd put as much money into their product as they do their marketing . . ."

It's supposed to be an apology, I think.

The visitor leans forward then, away from the carousel.

"Do they like it, though?" he says, nodding sideways and keeping his lips thin, as if the sunglasses might be listening.

I swallow, try to smile with my eyes, and know suddenly that Paula was wrong, that this can't be our visitor.

And then I smile. Just a small one.

"I think they do, yes," I manage to get out, my cheeks hot with another sun.

The visitor bites his top lip, turns back to the sunglasses, and nods, keeps nodding, as if my lie, if it even is a lie—maybe they *do* like it—goes right to the very heart of the thing all right, and then he does the thing I've been waiting for, praying for: smiles with just one side of his face, a wry smile, telling me that, yes, this has all just been a test. That he understands—nobody could be expected to perform under these conditions, could they?

I blink an earnest thank you to him and then he's walking away, first to Men's Shoes, where he tries on the left foot of every loafer we have, then, as if he's suddenly remembered something about his car in the parking lot, he wanders out, pushing through the glass doors instead of waiting for the automatic one to open.

Exactly ten seconds after he's gone, I breathe out, let my hand start shaking, and look across the store on accident, to Lingerie. Paula's there, sitting on one of the formica blocks reserved for mannequins. The particular one she's by is wearing a red teddy with a tasteful half-robe cinched around it.

Paula doesn't see me, is just staring down through her tunnel of hair, at the carpet.

But I'm not a bad employee.

I mean, in Men's Shoes, the new guy with the short hair, he's crying out loud, has been reduced to real and actual tears in the wake of this visitor.

As self-imposed penance, I skip break, work through dinner, and, after clocking out, the stockboys already moving in in their dark blue jumpsuits to reconfigure the store for the next visit, I purposefully walk by Lingerie, say it as I'm passing Paula—*I'm sorry*—and see what I couldn't from across the store: it's not Paula at all, but another mannequin. One dressed in Paula's clothes.

I don't break stride, though—you can't, at times like this—just nod to myself, roll the top of my purse over and leave through the warehouse, my heels clacking on the smooth concrete like I think they usually do. The only difference is that this time I see that the boxes, our supplies, our merchandise, the stuff from Corporate, it's all the same, box after box, shelf after shelf, receding in each direction for what looks like miles, so that I have to look away, control my breathing. Pretend I haven't seen anything here.

The way I smile is the way you smile when you're about to call yourself some private name that nobody else knows, but then I blink more than I mean to, have to reach out to a shelf for support, and, just in case this isn't a dream, the rest of the way out of the warehouse—years, miles, a lifetime—I drag my finger through the dust on the cardboard, leaving an up and down line that, the world willing, I should be able to follow back to the floor tomorrow, and all the other tomorrows I can already feel stacking up ahead of me.

THE CASE AGAINST HUMANITY

While the aliens had Gretchen and were using her to infiltrate other camps and kill everybody in their sleep, her roots grew back in, dark. Because mirrors weren't part of our day anymore, or our lives, she had no idea. It was hilarious.

When she walked around in that shuffling, post-inhabitation daze, Molly or Nicholas would fall in behind her, holding yellow grass at the tips of their brown hair, and it was all we could do not to fall over in laughter.

Finally, one night when the half-bombs (we didn't know what the aliens called them) were arcing across the sky, pulsing red and pale green, trying to sniff us out, Lancelot—he won't tell us his real name, claims it died with the earth—he reached across and held his hand over her stiff blonde ends, as if shielding them from aerial detection.

Without looking across to him, she put her hand over his, her fingertips cupping her right shoulder, and the look on her face, we could tell: she was thankful. To be, for the moment anyway, not so alone in this apocalypse.

Lancelot was nearly crying from the not-laughter, and probably would have exploded into hysterics, giving us all away, if a bomb hadn't drifted down into our midst.

Half the camp was neutralized, turned to that gooey kind of ash, and the rest of us found each other days later, miles away, our faces haggard, eyes dull.

By now Gretchen had an honest-to-goodness brown *stripe* down the middle of her head, where her not-blonde hair naturally fell into a part.

In our tents we whispered that it was like she'd got run over by a gravity-defying unicyclist who had just pedaled through a mud puddle. We said that she'd just ducked a bullet from the chocolate bandit. We said it was like she was cracking open, like she was going to climb her head with her fingers to that natural color and pull her brittle hair and surely-dry scalp apart, wiggle up a new person, one with darker hair.

That last one was kind of right.

Three days into our plodding trek to the mountains, where the bombs were supposed to get confused, miscounting the trees as people, Gretchen turned on her way to the central fire and caught Tang—definitely not his real name—aping her walk, eight inches of an old innertube laid across the center of his head like a rubbery Mohawk.

She stared him down exactly like she was waiting for her eyes to focus, for her mind to process, and then she nodded, continued on her way, biding her time until that night.

Instead of unfolding a scavenged coat hanger and burrowing it into our ears while we slept, or hovering over us mouth-to-mouth, breathing our breaths up before we could have them, what she did was walk out into the open right when the yellow grass was pulsing red and pale green, red and pale green. Life and death, life and death.

She waved twice to the bomb, then three times, and it shifted in the sky towards us.

We were almost to the mountains, too.

They were bald on top, studded with trees in a ring all around, like an old man's last lingering wreath of hair.

We'd been calling it Comb-Over Peak.

It was a good name.

I don't know what the aliens will call it.

HELL ON THE HOMEFRONT TOO

War changes a man. So does getting shot seventeen times by Germans. What Sandy had been hoping the War would change her husband Letch into was a dead man. Just so his outsides could match his insides. Or so his insides could be out. But seventeen German bullets wasn't enough. Letch came back to Decatur, Georgia a hero. As far as the town—America—was concerned, he was a miracle of science, too tough to die. Sandy knew different. He'd come back for her. And, now that he was who he was, the deputies weren't going to come out to the house anymore to stop him, she knew. Getting shot seventeen times was going to be his license to keep on doing to her what he'd already been doing for two years before Germany.

The day his bus rolled into town, Decatur PD caught her in Tallahassee, driving a truck she'd stolen from her uncle that morning. She was in her nightgown.

"You don't understand what he's like," she told Sheriff Karlson.

He laughed and delivered her back to Letch. Standing on the porch in his pants and undershirt, Letch saluted the sheriff then balled that same hand up, slung it into Sandy's face.

She crashed back into the clapboard wall.

Another Friday night in Georgia.

* * *

Two weeks later she didn't even recognize herself. Mostly Letch just hit her in the face, because it was hard to cook with broken arms, hard to clean with cracked ribs. They knew this from before the War.

"Make any friends while I was gone?" Letch asked from the kitchen table.

Sandy was standing at the sink, her bloodied nose dripping into the dishwater. This because she'd opened his beer instead of letting him do it himself.

"Just waiting for you," she said back.

Letch smiled, laughed through his nose.

The bullet holes had left puckers all along his left side, and gouged out some of his jaw line, made a furrow he was always touching now. What Sandy thought was that he wanted them to match, now—wanted to make her face like his. What she asked him while he was passed out in the living room wasn't *Why didn't you die?* but *How can you still be alive?*

She was talking to herself, of course.

The one time he caught her watching him sleep his finger jerked up to the scar on his cheek, and then he sat up, and Sandy knew that running wasn't any good, but she couldn't help it. She was in her nightgown again. He caught her by the mailbox and pushed her hard enough into it that her collarbone snapped. The metal also peeled some of the skin from her face. It flapped under her eye. She tried to hold it in place but Letch set his lips, knocked her hand down, then stepped back to hit her right there on the cheek.

Sandy didn't wake until morning. A dog was running its tongue all the way into her sinus cavity, it felt like. She rolled over onto her good side, threw up, and staggered inside. In the mirror, after rubbing it with alcohol, she could see the eggshell white of her cheekbone. She held her skin in place over it and knew better than to cry, because the salt from her tears would burn.

Letch didn't come back from the bars for three days after that, and when he did it was just because his hand was making him sick. He made Sandy work on it with a pair of pliers. What she finally pulled out, she was pretty sure, was a splinter of bone from her cheek. It was too late, though. The hand was already infected, red streaks of blood poisoning climbing Letch's arm.

She rolled his sleeve down to his wrist, told him he'd be fine.

The next time he came home was a week later.

His hand smelled like rot, and his arm was going black.

"Does it hurt?" Sandy asked him.

"Looking at you, y'mean?" he said back.

This time she spit on the bandage before cleaning his hand.

Four days later, her collarbone starting to mend, Letch crashed his truck into the porch. The whole house shook.

Sandy pulled him from behind the wheel, opened his shirt. The rot—gangrene?—was all the way across his chest now, but, like in Germany, he still wouldn't die. She touched the skin and it was spongy, like meat that'd been in the sun too long. She left him there for the flies, and they came, blanketed him, but still his chest rose and fell. On the third day, no food, no beer, he coughed, turned his head to the side, and retched maggots onto the shoulder of his shirt.

Sandy sat on the porch and watched, a warm cloth on her collarbone.

"Seventeen times," she said to herself, and lit a candle to mask the smell of decay.

* * *

By the ninth day, Letch's whole body was black like he'd burned, and this time when he opened his mouth, full-grown bottle-flies drifted up.

"You're dead," Sandy told him, from the porch.

Letch's shoulders hitched together and then he coughed, and it turned into a laugh. He pulled himself up with the bumper of the truck.

"Not so long as I got my baby," he told her, and lurched onto the porch railing.

Sandy stepped back, her eyes flared wide.

"Lay down, William Letch Cross," she said, trying her best to sound like a preacher.

"On top of you . . ." he said back, smiling, then pulled himself up onto the porch faster than she would have thought he could, being dead and all.

Up close he smelled even worse.

She pushed him away, ran inside, but he caught her by the hair, slammed her into the china closet. She fell holding her collarbone in place, started crawling then. Letch walked behind her, like he just wanted to see where she was going.

"Yeah," he said, when she got to the stove, "that's right, baby. Daddy's hungry."

Sandy pulled herself up the door, to the burner, to the iron skillet her mother had left her. It was full of pork chop grease, still melted from breakfast. She slung it back onto Letch. He licked it off his face with his purple tongue, started fingering the rest in, his white, lidless eyes fixed on her.

"Not quite K-rations," he said, "but who am I to complain, right?"

"How many times you say you got shot over there?" Sandy asked.

Letch stopped licking the grease and just stared at her, said it: "Seventeen."

"Guess they don't know you like I do," Sandy said, and brought the match around, scratching the head on her belt.

Letch went up like a torch. When he still wouldn't die, Sandy started in on him with the backside of the pan, and, because he was still laughing, trying to, she went outside for the axe, came back, left him in pieces. Just to be sure, she burned them too, until he was crumbs and ash and bits of bone. This she funneled into a tall metal thermos, the one Letch had come back from the War with. And then, her eyes closed tight, she reset her collarbone.

Two days later, at a diner in Tallahassee, all her clothes in the bed of her uncle's truck, the waitress bellied up to her side of the counter, an order pad in her hand.

"You okay, darling?" she said.

Sandy just stared at a dirty spot on the counter.

"Anybody comes asking for me—" she said.

The waitress narrowed her eyes, waiting.

"I went . . . I went west," Sandy finally finished.

"West," the waitress said, tapping her pencil on her pad. "Not down to Miami, right?"

Sandy bit her lower lip, nodded.

"He that bad?" the waitress said.

Sandy squeezed her eyes shut.

"California it is, then," the waitress said, shrugging, then, after one of the men in the far booths started tapping his spoon on the side of his water glass, she came back to Sandy, held up a stained pot, asked, "How you like your coffee there, Hon?"

Sandy focused in on the thermos she'd brought in with her. It was sitting by the napkin dispenser.

"Like I like my men," she said, a new hardness in her eyes, like laughter.

"Black?" the waitress asked back, a lilt in her voice because she'd heard the joke.

"No," Sandy said, shaking her head, touching her collarbone, "in a cup."

I WAS A TEENAGE SLASHER VICTIM

You're riding in the car with your mom when she kind of shudders in a way you think you're not supposed to see, grips the wheel harder, and adjusts the rearview mirror away from you.

It's night, late, maybe even midnight. You can't see the clock from your seatbelt.

Once before you've stayed up past midnight, but that was when your Uncle Dani wrecked her motorcycle and you had to eat dinner from a dollar-machine in the hall and everybody was crying.

You're ten, say.

It's a Friday, almost Halloween.

Where your mom's driving you is the long way to your dad's new house. It's supposed to be a surprise visit, an early trick 'r treat.

But now she's crying.

"Mom?" you say, leaning forward as far as you can without breaking the seatbelt rule.

She shakes her head no, nothing.

A few roads later she adjusts the mirror back to you.

"What is it?" you ask, and can hear it in your voice, that her crying is trying to spread to you.

She can hear it too.

"I was—I was just thinking about when I was . . . a long time ago. I don't know why."

"When you were my age?"

"When I met your father."

"High school," you say, because you know the story of where they met: summer camp at the lake with the complicated name.

She nods too fast. Rubs her nose with the back of her hand.

"Tell me again," you say.

It's comfortable, this story. It's canoes and sloppy joes in a pot big enough to hold a dog (that's the joke every year), and it's sneaking out at night to swim, which you're never supposed to do but everybody does.

Your mom clicks her headlights to bright—there hasn't been another car for longer than it usually takes to even *get* to your dad's—and nods her head like okay. Like this is good. Like she can do this.

It's the same kind of nod you do in your room when you've built cities of blocks and are about to walk through them slow, so you can watch each building crash into the next building, and do the sounds with your mouth. It's from the monster movies your dad watches with you on Saturday mornings. But he never understands them right, he always thinks the monsters are from bombs or from the ocean or from some scientist.

You know, though. The reason they're so strong is they've got future muscles. *Every*body where they come from can breathe fire.

How else could it be?

As for why the big split between her and your dad, it's pretty much the usual mystery, except one fight you heard the end of was something about a door being closed. How she should have known right then and right there. And your dad saying no, that he was sorry, that he could fix it, he could make it up.

That he would do it right now if she wanted, he would walk right in there with the axe or a bowling ball or whatever and he would—

After that, at night, you checked all the doors in the house, with everybody sleeping. That's what the fight had been about.

They all worked perfectly. Except maybe your mom and dad's, but that one was locked like always. Like they're scientists in there, trying to cook up a monster but embarrassed about it.

Your friend Trace says that when his parents fight, one of them always sleeps on the couch.

Not at your house.

"We were seventeen," your mom says from the front seat, and you close your eyes, are there with her again, seeing summer camp through her eyes.

Except this time there's more.

Your mom's so young, and she looks at her knees a lot.

She's a counselor. Her and your dad, in his short shorts with the two stripes on the side like a green racetrack.

Don't laugh.

They don't know each other yet, even.

The game your dad used to play with you in your room—it's nothing bad—it was for the two of you to dress up from the costume box (clowns, pirates, alligator heads) to look at their old pictures from the album. But to see them right you had to look through the frame of the mirror from the hall you'd accidentally broke, that had all the mirror gone now, and the back part as well. Your dad would lean the brown frame up against the wall and then put the picture album down under it, and always be careful to reach around to turn the pages. He said this was how you looked into the past.

So, when you close your eyes to see him and your mom at

camp, the sky all golden and dusty every day, it's like your dad's sitting there beside you with a pirate patch over his eye.

Looking at the old pictures started when your dog Philip (you chose the name) had to go live with people in the country, so he could run and be free and have a better life.

It was like trading Philip for summer camp. And it was a good trade.

Your mom and dad didn't take pictures of everything, though.

Because your mom knows you know all the normal parts, she doesn't go through them this time. They've told you all about the archery, about the tire swing into the lake. About how the moose head in the cafeteria was supposed to be haunted, and about how, the last night there was bonfire night, and that that was when your dad first put his arm around your mom, with all those sparks leaking up into the sky, never coming down.

Those are the parts you want, but now there's more parts.

This time there's the accident with the arrow. That's what your mom calls it from the front seat.

Through her eyes or her words, you can't tell anymore, you see it: the newest counselor, the one who just walked up, hasn't even checked in yet. He's behind the big hay targets. Not accidentally shot once, maybe in the eye because that would be deadliest, but shot twelve times, all in the face. From somebody who had to have been standing right over him. Standing on his arms probably.

"His head was a—it was a *pin*cushion," your mom says all at once, the crying back in her voice. And she tried to lift him up but couldn't, because he was stuck by the head to the ground.

By the time she pulled everybody back to the archery range, the dead counselor was gone gone gone. Not even any blood.

They counted the arrows and there was one quiverful missing, but nobody took your mom's screaming seriously. Not even your dad.

Then, next, two counselors who had been kissing in the shut-down showers—all your mom can get out before her voice breaks down, it's blood, swirling around the super-rusted drain. Then clumping. And there was hair on the wall, maybe. Hair that wasn't attached anymore.

And—this makes her lose the car's direction, scatter gravel up from the ditch—this time she saw someone running off. Or she heard them, fast feet, and built a shadow up from there.

But how tall? What kind of hair? Did it look back at her while it was running away?

And then the girl who had been killed in the shower, had had things done to her chest area, had her hair already smeared on the wall, she grabbed her hand onto your mom's ankle.

Your mom screamed, kicked away.

"It was . . . it's—it's," the girl managed to say, then conked, something black like coffee pouring out one side of her mouth.

Before your mom could get your dad back to those shut-down restrooms (he'd been fiberglassing the slow canoe for the next day), the shut-down restrooms suddenly burned down like they were made of hay bales and gasoline.

It was like bonfire night, too early.

The owners of the camp sprayed it with water, then, in the morning, put yellow tape all around it, because the place was dangerous. They said the two dead counselors had really just left to go home, and the fire, it was probably campers smoking cigarettes Or smoking something.

When they said that 'something,' your dad's hand squeezed your mom's harder, like he was scared.

Meaning they lied, about him putting his arm around her for the first time on that last night.

This is the real story, the secret story.

You're almost holding your breath.

* * *

The next day was normal, just the usual canoe races, the counselor hiding with snorkel tubes after the finish line, to tump everybody over, winners and all.

Except one of those campers, when she came back up, it was with a dead body draped over her like moss.

It was one of the owners, the wife. Her eyes had been sewed shut, her mouth cut too wide, all the skin and meat cut from her fingerbones.

Then the owner who was the husband floated up, floating like a log with eyes.

After getting everybody to shore and turning their screaming into whimpering, your dad tried to start all the cars but none of them had any battery. And the telephones were all dead.

Your mom and dad did important eyes to each other about all of this. Scared eyes.

Everybody camped in the cafeteria, even though all the walls were windows. They kept all the lights on. They watched the moose in shifts.

Two more nights, then the purple bus would show back up.

In the front seat, your mom's not trying not to cry anymore.

"You were so brave," you tell her.

This makes her cry harder.

"We didn't know who it was!" she says, hitting her hand onto the steering wheel. "We thought it had to be one of us, though. Right? Right?"

You nod, are liking this story. The past is an interesting place.

That night, most of the littler kids asleep, your dad outside so he can smoke one of his cigarettes, all the lights suddenly suck back into their light bulbs, and won't turn back on.

In the darkness, a small hand takes your mom's hand.

She screams, shakes the hand off.

When they finally get some candles going, it turns out the hand she shook off was one of the littler kids', the one who's always been scared the whole time, even before the dead bodies. He's crying in the corner, asking for his mom, and the way he's scared of your dad means he's scared of his own dad too.

It makes your mom from back then cry, and she's crying when she's talking about crying, too. How much she hated herself. How mad it made her, that a kid's dad would hurt him. And that now she was like that dad, hurting the kid too.

So they decided to do something about this.

The next morning, instead of hiding, they tried to do the usual camp stuff, just always staying with a buddy.

Only, what whoever was doing this didn't know—unless it was one of them—was that each counselor had a weapon hidden in their shirt or their pants.

Your dad had a fireplace poker. Your mom had one of the knives from the high shelf.

Their idea was to lure this person out, then do something to him.

"But it only happens at night, right?" you say.

Your mom doesn't answer.

The kids all line up for the tire swing, your dad shimmying (he's so *skinny*) out onto the big branch, to make sure there's nothing wrong with the rope, or the limb.

It's all just normal.

He nods and one of the other counselors secretly hands his little baseball bat to the other counselor and rears back on the tire swing, holding it the way the old kids get to, and runs for the water with it.

He goes out high, higher, then lets go at the perfect time, reaching up for the sky with his feet like upside-down diving.

But your dad didn't check the lake.

Bobbing right there under this counselor is one of the triangle buoys, its orange and white stripes painted over, just a blue kind of black.

The counselor sees the top of that upside-down ice-cream cone coming for him, and he flaps and twists and screams.

It doesn't matter.

It goes in through his stomach, splashes up through his back.

On shore, kids and counselors scatter everywhere.

The only two counselors now are your mom and your dad.

And, "And we didn't think it was a *kid* doing it," your mom says, her eyes in the mirror so red by now.

You're peeking.

Don't.

But you see it anyway, on the side of the road.

It's a man, tall like your dad. Like he's asking for a ride.

Your mom takes her foot off the gas so the car's coasting, so quiet, and, just when the headlights are about to touch the man, show who he is, she clicks the headlights off.

You twist around, see his shape in the brake lights anyway, when your mom's still thinking about stopping.

He's got a fireplace poker.

"I don't even know where all the kids *went*," your mom says, lighting the road back up.

"Is Philip out here?" you say to her, because this can't be the way to your dad's house, and she laughs and cries at the same time, like a cough that hurts.

Because some of the kids go back to their assigned bunk-houses to hide in their beds, under the covers, your mom and dad go there too.

They have their weapons out in the open now.

And, that one little kid who the whole time at camp has been trying to tell your mom about a ghost he's been seeing at night, the one who tried to hold your mom's hand in the cafeteria when the lights went out, he shows her the pictures he's been drawing.

They're mostly about the mouth. Red and evil. Teeth like little gravestones.

Your mom holds that kid close, sees her own face reflected in the trembly blade of her knife.

That night, instead of candles, they do the bonfire. Right on schedule.

Everybody sits close enough to it (your dad holding your mom close, your mom leaning into him) that they don't see the big shadowy person standing behind them, just watching.

Whoever it is shines his light from face to face, everybody screaming inside, too scared to run.

It's just the sheriff, though.

The kids pile onto his legs like puppies, and he lets them.

Finally he settles his flashlight on your mom and dad. His light bright on your mom's knife.

"What's going on here?" he says.

Your mom swallows, the sound loud in her ears.

Why the sheriff's there is that one of the kids' cousins was getting called to the army, so that kid needed to go home, say bye in case that was the last time to say it.

But he never expected this.

"Where's Ralph and Laurie?" he says, his light up on your mom's face now.

Your dad hooks his head out to the lake like he's sorry and the sheriff steps over there as best he can, with kids all over him, and shines his light on the three bodies in the lake: the owners at the edge, the counselor on the buoy.

He wades through the kids, back to his car.

Only, when he starts to scream something into his radio, a hand pulls his forehead back against his seat, and another hand, from the other side, drags a shiny knife across his throat like just drawing a line in Jell-O.

His blood burbles out onto his light brown shirt, and, when he falls forward, he pushes the sirens on.

The kids scream, everybody's screaming, running through the red lights flashing everywhere, and your mom runs for the Chestnuts bunkhouse because it's closest, but your dad's already there, pulling the door shut behind him and pushing the wooden peg in to lock it.

She beats on it with her fists and stabs it with her knife but your dad's in the bathroom already, hiding in the bathtub. Except the bathtub's where that one artist kid has been leaving all his paintings, so it's like the killer or the ghost is in there with him already.

Your mom finally crawls in through the window right over him, falls down onto him even though he locked her out, and somehow he doesn't stab her with his poker and she doesn't cut him with her knife, and they hide like that until the bus shows up, and then get married and love each other and have you someday.

But: "Who was it?" you ask.

"The—the artist kid's dad," your mom says.

They found him trapped in a complicated trap at the edge of the woods. It was a hole with broken paddles on the bottom, splinter-side-up. He had blood all over them, and his mouth was painted red just like his son had been drawing. Because the dad was a clown for parties.

"He got caught in one of his own things," your mom said, looking to you like you're supposed to nod.

You don't, though.

* * *

What you're trying to think is how could your dad know about the Sheriff getting cut like that across the throat if he was already in the Chestnuts bunkhouse?

But your mom must have seen it, told him.

Right?

But now your mom's all over the road, and there are no lights at all out here.

"Was that Dad back there?" you ask.

"*It's too late!*" she screams about your question, and spills her purse onto the seat beside her, isn't even driving anymore, is just scratching for something.

She pushes it back to you.

You uncrumple it—it's old paper—and you kind of have to smile.

It's one of the artist kid's drawings. She must have saved it all this time.

"We're going to see Philip, yes," she says, and hunches over the wheel like somebody just hit her in the stomach. "You'll like it there, it'll be . . . right."

You see her eyes in the mirror for a moment but she pulls them away. Like she's scared.

Clowns.

It's what the kid was drawing.

Only—only it's not a dad at all.

When you were dressed like this, your dad was wearing a pirate patch on his eye.

Not you.

You always liked the big wig, the funny nose, the red mouth. That scratchy collar that was like paper folded over and over. The floppy shoes that made that sound when you ran.

Maybe that's how your mom figured it out.

Maybe she heard you running in the hall. And remembered.

But it's not your fault, even. Some days your dad, he forgets to put the mirror frame up, doesn't he? Just leaves it leaning there. And, without him to tell you not to, instead of reaching around like he taught, you can reach right through for that perfect magic summer camp. You're even small enough to *step* through. To be there with them in the album. To watch them from the edges of the woods. From the dock, at night.

And you were right about future muscles.

"It's you," your mom says, her body all-the-way pressed to the door, like she wants to be as far away as possible.

You lean over so you can see her in the mirror again.

She's trying to hide.

You smile, feel the paint crackle around your mouth.

It's how she found you earlier, in your room. Already dressed up.

Paint on your hands too, but that's not paint.

"I was just playing," you tell her. "Are we really going to see Philip?"

She nods yes, yes yes yes, that's *right* where you're going, and you nod, look out the side window at the shadows of fence posts blurring together.

But there's something in the floorboard, too.

It's peeking out from under the seat, where you hid it.

The thick black blade from your dad's lawnmower. The one he threw away.

You nod, look out the side window again.

Your heart's thumping like a rabbit now.

Go ahead, lift the blade with your toe so it meets your hand, know that your dad won't catch up this far for ten or thirty minutes.

It'll be just like camp. The best one ever.

You smile, lean forward, breaking the seatbelt rule but the seatbelt rule doesn't matter anymore.

Your mom, though. She's been through all this before, hasn't she? She doesn't just remember the bad parts, she remembers how to live, too. She opens her door, rolls out into the darkness, and, one hand on the back of the front seat, you see the road about to turn in front of you, but there's nobody to turn the wheel anymore. To keep up with the road.

"Philip," you say, right at the end.

It was the artist kid's name. The one who wouldn't ever go to sleep. The one who would never come out into the woods to play.

When the car hits whatever it hits, you launch over the front seat, and it's just like letting go of a tire swing at the exact perfect right time. Especially when you see that the window's already breaking. The glass is going away, getting ready for you.

Leaving only the frame it was in.

You're just small enough to slip through it without touching it, even with the back of your clown shoe. Just small enough to crash into the water of the past, like always.

You stand from it, the water dripping off the lawnmower blade you still have.

Right now the camp's empty, deserted, lonely.

But it won't always be.

THE MANY STAGES OF GRIEF

THE CONVERSATION JIM HAD FIRST THING MONDAY MORNING:

"So what happened to your face there?"

It was Kate talking.

Jim raised his hand to the ragged side of his face, shrugged, told her some truth: "While my two year old son thinks it hilarious for me to pretend to eat from the dog's bowl, the dog doesn't see the humor."

"It looks like a knife fight."

"Labrador teeth."

"Or your face caught on fire and someone tried to put it out with a hatchet."

"Is Smithson paying you to be this extra-funny?"

"When does the eye patch come off, captain?"

Never.

Jim was a monocular dad now. That he might need depth perception to properly raise his son was having absolutely no bearing on whether he would get to *have* depth perception. Maybe his ears would compensate, though?

He could hear Kate grinning all the way down the hall.

THE CONVERSATION JIM HAD WITH HIS WIFE AT 9:00 BREAK:

"Hello?"

Jim put a question mark there because she hadn't spoken into the phone yet.

"I'm in the *car*, dear."

"Just one question then."

"One."

"The other day when I asked if you liked my new basketball shoes, do you remember?"

"Yes. That's your question?"

"No. You looked at them and said you just can't seem to get into the new style."

"And?"

"What were you saying?"

"You can't play basketball anymore, Jim, heart. Sorry to have to be the one to tell you."

"That's just what you want, isn't it?"

"You think he's watching, but he's not. Are you listening?"

No.

Yes.

'He' was the new neighbor across the street, one house to the right. The new high school coach. He watered the lawn in polyester coach shorts; looped over his rearview mirror was a gold-plated whistle and a stop-watch.

He was watching, all right. Jim could tell.

*THE CONVERSATION JIM HAD OVER LUNCH WITH LARRY,
JUST RECENTLY PROMOTED:*

"I just saw it in the paper, the supplement. I don't know all the details."

Larry read all the papers. It was his job, now.

"But it was a dolphin?"

"The old man just moseyed out for the morning paper or to watch the college girls across the street jiggle to their car or whatever, and there it was."

"The dolphin."

"*Breathing*, man. That's the thing. In Boulder, Colofreakingrado, get it? The foothills of the Rocky Mountains?"

Jim looked up like the old man had to have, for an explanation, for where this *fish* could have come from, and Larry stood into that space: "They think it was this kidnapped dolphin. Like the kidnappers ran out of water or the owners wouldn't pay anything but market price."

"But they *ate* it?"

"It's a delicacy. It died in their bathtub. They tried to use rock salt to make seawater."

"Yeah," Jim said, "rock salt," and after Larry was gone he monocu-lared in on his own thumbnail clicking on the table top, saying in dolphinspeak *please, please help me*. No one in upper management wears a patch. They don't even wear eyeglasses up there.

*THE CONVERSATION JIM HAD WITH HIS LABRADOR (TAD)
WHEN HE HAD GOTTEN HOME FROM THE HOSPITAL
THAT NIGHT AFTER THE DOG FOOD:*

"I know it wasn't your fault, bub."

Jim the Forgiver. The understanding human in the room.

Tad thumped his tail on the floor in appreciation.

"But did you have to do it so deep? I mean, isn't there supposed to be a growl, then maybe a feint, *then* a snap? Don't they teach you this at dog-school? You have to admit it was funny, though. Brent, you saw him, Brent was even still laughing when, when my, you know, when you—" but then Jim couldn't finish, couldn't describe in words his eyeball in the dog food, the dark pupil contracting in fear.

THE CONVERSATION JIM HAD WITH HIS WIFE MARGARET ON THE DRIVE HOME FROM THE HOSPITAL THAT NIGHT:

"Thank you."

"You would have done the same thing."

"I wouldn't have known to."

"He was just protecting his food, you know."

It's what she's been saying all day already.

"But . . . Brent."

It's also what she's been saying. Brent. Brent Brent Brent.

"I know, I know. But couldn't you have just like lured him away with some people food?"

"It was an emergency. That's what the taser's *for*, an emergency. I mean, we had to get your eye, right? There was still a chance."

Jim rubbed his hollow eye socket.

"I know."

"But you think it scarred him psychologically?"

"Brent?"

"Brent? *Tad.*"

"Tad, yeah. He's going to be scared of all handheld devices

now, don't you think? I mean, I'll pull out a calculator to help Brent with his homework, and—"

"He's got the taste of blood, now."

Margaret looked across the seat at Jim, importantly.

"I'll talk to him," Jim said, but what he wasn't saying was Did she really have to use the taser on *him*, too? He hadn't been that out of control, had he? In front of Brent, in the backyard, where the whole neighborhood could hear?

THE CONVERSATION JIM AND MARGARET OFTEN HAVE ABOUT BRENT:

"It doesn't look like a diaper bag. It looks like a purse."

Jim isn't lying. They're at the grocery store, checking out, or standing in line for a movie that's a compromise.

"Can you just hold it while I write the check, please? Just for a moment?"

"That you used it as a purse before we had a . . . before we had Brent. It doesn't help any here, you know."

"It doesn't look like a purse."

"You *wear* it like a purse, though. Your lipstick's in there. I say anything with lipstick in it's a purse."

"Would you just hold it for a moment, Jim? Please?"

"Men don't carry purses."

"Keep your elbow straight. Hold it as far away from you as possible. That'll tell anybody looking that you're a manly man. That you watch football and drink beer and play poker and smoke cigars all at once."

"How much is the check for?"

"This is just like when you call me from work. Brent's crying now, okay?"

"What's that he's wearing anyway? Is that a shirt or a dress?"

Margaret cries too much, really, Jim suspects. And draws far too many suicide-pictures. In one series of them she's hanging from a bouquet of balloons by the neck, floating away dead (eyes X'd) from Jim, lying on the floor with a kitchen knife in his eye. These pictures were all before the dog food day, too, before the hospital night. Jim says it wasn't coincidence, *can't* be. His therapist is inclined to agree.

THE CONVERSATION JIM HAD WITH HIS THERAPIST ON THE WAY HOME FROM WORK:

"I'm in traffic, see? That was just a real, live honking horn."

"Are they honking at you, Jim?"

"Do you have to say my name so much, *doctor*? Is there like somebody else on the other line, is that it? You just trying to keep us straight or something?"

"One question at a time, Jim. You know the rule."

"Okay then, *doctor*. Your honest, expert opinion now. Do I have a chance?"

"Of making the team?"

"Yes."

"You're thirty-four years old, Jim."

"I'm in good shape, though. Hear that? That's how my stomach sounds when I hit it. I can pick which calf muscle to push the accelerator with."

"And you're not really enrolled in high school, either. That might be the big thing."

"But if I was?"

"You're not, though, Jim."

"Then why does he watch me?"

"Why do *you* think he watches you?"

"You're trying to make this about my eye, aren't you?"

"Which one, Jim?"

Jim hung up with his thumb. He knew why his new neighbor was watching him: nostalgia, for what never was—him and Jim, coach and player, sweeping state two years in a row, Jim's junior and senior years, the time of his life he never had. That neither of them ever had.

Jim held the wheel with both hands and misjudged the light, pulled a half car-length into the intersection and held his place, making everyone go around him.

THE SHORT CONVERSATION JIM HAD WITH HIS FAMILY OVER DINNER (CHICKEN):

"Is that dog food in your okra?"

Jim looked to Brent to see if Brent had heard this accusation from mother to father. Brent had; his fork was stopped halfway up for the rest of his childhood. Jim turned back to Margaret.

"Have you been looking at my food again?"

"I can smell it, Jim."

"Jim? What about *dear, heart, love of my life, father of my only son*?"

"Jim."

"Yes, okay. It's dog food. It's perfectly nutritional."

"Does Tad know?"

This was Brent in a small voice, peering up.

Jim closed his one good eye.

No, Tad didn't know. Jim had distracted him with an open gate and a fake meow then sneaked a pocketful. It was therapy. Nobody was supposed to know, though.

THE CONVERSATION JIM HAD WITH LARRY WHEN HE ASKED HIM OVER TO PLAY BASKETBALL AFTER DINNER:

"You really want me to *wear* this thing?"

The extra eye patch.

"Yes."

"This going to get kinky?"

Jim shook his head no.

"It's just to even things up some. You can play without depth perception, you know."

"Should I give myself a quick frontal lobotomy too, captain? Develop some peculiar neuroses? What about those shoes, though. Did you buy them just for this?"

"I needed new shoes. Don't look at them please."

"*Pret*-ty."

In the kitchen window Brent and Margaret were receding in Jim's vision, small like at the end of a telescope.

Across the street a set of blinds fingered open.

Jim smiled, bounced the ball to Larry.

"To eleven. Make it take it."

Larry dribbled the ball once with both hands, testing it, and smiled.

"Like always," he said, pulling it back by his waist, his triple threat position.

Jim nodded and crouched over in his defensive stance, palms up, and spread his finger, waiting.

THE CONVERSATION JIM HAD WITH KATE AGAIN TUESDAY MORNING:

"So what happened now?"

"Nothing."

"But you used to have teeth, didn't you? I think I remember teeth, definitely."

"It was a last second shot. A buzzer beater."

"And your ankle. It didn't used to have all that stuff on it, did it?"

"It doesn't matter."

"I hope you won, at least?" and Jim grinned into Kate's cubicle, told her some truth: that Brent had been watching. That of course he had won. His new neighbor had even come out onto his lawn to watch at the end, and then flag down the ambulance.

"He told me I made the team," Jim whispered. "That I was good enough."

"You were bleeding, though. You still are."

"And I stayed awake until the paramedics—" but then he could hear the tears forming in her eyes and had to look away, hold his breath against the salty smell. The office wasn't the place for that kind of emotion. Smithson had warned him about it, even, but still, hobbling away from her with a noisy grin Jim felt the tears on his *own* face—on *both* sides—and finally breathed in, made his office in two great vaults of his crutches, then only leaned on them for a moment with his head down before reaching for the phone, to ask Margaret if she'd ever heard of a human eye growing back. Because he could feel it in there like a pearl, perfect and unborn.

CATCH AND RELEASE

"My dad used to take me there all the time when I was young."

"Oh, this one again."

"I'm not making it up."

"Of course not. My dad used to take me to magic fishing holes all the time when I was kid, too. It's part of growing up, isn't it?"

"This was real."

"I'm sure it was. To you."

"I'm going to find it again."

"It's out there, it's out there."

"Sure, make fun."

"Listen. You miss your dad, I get that. And don't take this wrong. But there aren't any places that good. Never were."

"Except I was there."

"Look, he's getting all dreamy again."

"All you need is a light. They come right to it. Every time. It's like they can't help themselves."

"'It's like they *wanted* to get caught . . .' Any of them ever just climb in on their own?"

"They would have, yeah. It's like—like we were saving them. You could see it in their eyes."

"You can see what you want to see. I believe that."

"Yeah, okay. But, serious, it was like they were thinking. Like they were trying so hard to think. Like they were just almost there."

"And then they saw you."

"They were so helpless, you know?"

"How could they serve your god-complex if they weren't?"

"No, it's like they wanted to trust us. It would be kind of perfect at first, one of them looking at me. Me looking right at it. But then their bodies would take over. Their natural responses. From not breathing, I guess."

"You *guess*?"

"What do we look like to them, you think?"

"You talking about what do we look like to your made-up ones, or to real ones?"

"I don't even know why I talk to you."

"No, I'm with you here. All the way. I mean, no, of course no place like that really ever actually *existed*, we'd have all heard about it, but—"

"I think it's where my dad wrecked."

"He said dourly."

"Sorry. His ship, though—you know how he was. One more run."

"Without you."

"He probably knew it was going to leak. That it might. So he didn't wake me up to go with him."

"Then good for him, right?"

"What do you mean?"

"I mean he went to that perfect fishing hole in the sky, and he got to *stay*."

"No. I mean, it was good fishing, yeah. The best. But we never dipped down too low. He said if we fell in, that was it, it was over, done. They'd eat us alive."

"Eat?"

"As in destroy, infect, I don't know."

"What'd you use for bait?"

"The light was good to draw them in, like I was saying. They must not have enough of it or something. Or not the good kind. But we used all different stuff, I guess. My dad had one lure that looked like—I don't know what you'd call it. It had parts, was like a ship, I guess, but it only went on the ground, in a mostly straight line. If you left one just sitting there, though, it was like they couldn't help themselves."

"So they weren't thinkers, then. Good, good. Go on."

"Shut up."

"Serious. I want to hear. Regale me."

"Sometimes we'd use their . . . whatever they called them down there. The other ones like them but weren't them, that were bigger and slower. I think they grew them to eat them, maybe."

"Come on. If you're going to lie, then make it big. Entertain me."

"We'd find one of those and hollow it out, make it real dry, then just drop it down and wait."

"You tried that particular trick anywhere else since then?"

"Nowhere else has those to try with."

"But how would you reel them in, then?"

"That was the easy part. Just shift to the heavy light. It tranced them out or something. They'd just look up and up into it. And they didn't know how to phase—"

"I was almost believing you there."

"They didn't know. They don't."

"Then they'd be dead before they even started living. No species can survive without phasing. You'd just be locked in one view, right? I'd be trying to climb into your ship, too."

"I don't know, they found some way to keep on living. Maybe they didn't even know, thought what they could see, that that was everything. Like—just a lower level of existing, moment to moment, in one direction. And then it's over just all at once."

"So you *were* a god to them. For delivering them from that."

"Dad said that was what made them so special to catch. Pulling them up into the ship for an orbit or two, it made their lives so much bigger. At least for then."

"What do you mean?"

"They can't phase? When we'd lower them the *other* way through the light, time would go backwards for them, and it was like they couldn't even remember us."

"Now I know you're lying."

"It was sad. Dad said maybe if I marked them they could hold on to us some. I mean, in their heads."

"They're strictly organic, you're saying?"

"Exactly. The first few I marked—well. You know how it goes."

"They're fragile. Built to die. Sounds like they were already practically dead."

"I know. I was a kid, though, right? Dad, you know how he was, he could slap them against the wall when they made too much noise, easy as that. Not even think twice. Their heads were so delicate."

"A planet for every kind."

"We never told anybody about it, either. Everybody would have come, ruined it."

"But how'd you mark them if they came apart so easy?"

"I'd just stuff random bits from our toolbox in them. The natural openings. Just wherever I could, wherever it looked like something might fit."

"You didn't keep one, did you? Is that where this is going?"

"You can't eat them."

"Well."

"You *could*, okay. But believe me, you wouldn't want to."

"Especially when *you* got done with them."

"It wasn't on purpose. I was just playing."

"I'm joking, I'm joking. But you really think your dad went back in a leaky ship?"

"Whenever he'd be reeling one in, he'd always have me to watch the gravity for him, make sure we didn't fall in. I wasn't there for the last time, though. He probably hooked a big one, but there was nobody there to watch the panel. He would have crashed."

"Into the middle of a bunch of them. All with junk stuffed in them by his kid."

"I wonder if they remembered him then. Made the connection."

"'A magic place. They come right up to you. And they never remember, just keep coming back for more and more.'"

"I shouldn't have told you."

"Everybody likes a good lie."

"My dad didn't crashland into a lie."

"Just into a place without phasing. A place you can fish forever, reeling the same ones up, and they never know it."

"Okay."

"What?"

"This. Shh."

"What? It's all shriveled and black—oh, oh. It's one of them?"

"Part. It fell off."

"Hunh. Almost looks like a hand, except for those five . . . whatever they are."

"They use them as natural as anything, I swear."

"And I'm supposed to believe this is what they run their magical perfect planet with?"

"You can take them off and they don't die right away. Maybe because they come with an extra. Like a back-up."

"An extra?"

"They're bilateral."

"Oh, of course, of course. This is getting better and better. You should have stopped with stuffing your little pieces of junk into them."

"When we'd have them on the ship, some of them would use these—see, the five things kind of spread open? They would . . . I don't know what they were doing. But it looked like they were trying to reach for us somehow. Like they wanted to touch us. See if we were real."

"Defense mechanism. Probably a stinger or something in the middle, if you get too close."

"That's what Dad said."

"Listen, I am sorry. About him. I really hope he's out there still, just floating on their—you say they're breathers?"

"There's an atmosphere."

"I hope he's there, just dropping his light through it over and over, pulling them in and throwing them back as fast as he can."

"You know he is."

"Long live secret fishing holes."

"And fathers."

"And sons."

"And breathers who can't phase."

"And breathers who can't remember."

"And fishermen who do."

SUBMITTED FOR YOUR APPROVAL

It starts with a man walking back from the kitchen to his couch, a bowl of dry cereal in his hand, his other hand in the bowl, fingering out a bite or two. It's not that he doesn't have milk, just that he could hear the opening credits—his own sultry sly voice—and suddenly didn't have time for milk anymore. Again. This is maybe four years after production stopped, the Show already looped into the afterlife of syndication. And this man, this man with the dry cereal pinched halfway to his mouth, is none other than Mr. Rod Serling, no suit, no tie, but still, him, alone enough this evening to forego milk altogether, just sit back on the couch and try to resist touching his hair when he sees himself on the television set, touching it as if to fix it.

This evening, however, he only makes it halfway across the living room.

He lowers his hand from his mouth, doesn't chew the cereal because it's dry, would crunch, and he has to hear.

Someone on the porch?

Maybe.

In the moment before he moves to the door, the bowl of cereal balanced on the tall back cushion of the couch, he notes the curtains over the front window, open, and pictures somebody hunched over there, watching him watch the Show. He wonders what kind of thrill that would be—wonders if he would do that himself, and what the difference would be between watching himself on television and watching himself watching himself on television—and like that another Episode flashes across his mind, of a man stepping into a public bathroom, getting caught in the continually diminishing reflection of the mirrors to either side of him, until the reflection breaks down and, at five-eighths of an inch tall, he becomes someone else, someone independent of himself, smiling.

They had a good run, though. Even without touching on every possible script. He's learned to tell himself these things, anyway.

In two steps, then, he's at the door, is stepping out onto the wooden porch, into the twilit night. No one; nobody. Not even the neighbors, standing on their porches too, waiting for the aliens to land or not land. For a man to run silent down the street, his jacket on fire.

But—the sound, the noise, that distinctive shuffle of leather on wood planks.

Mr. Rod Serling closes the door, locks it, and only then does it register: *leather*. Leather soles. Dress shoes.

He looks to the side as he approaches his dry cereal, trying to build a man up from the bottom, from a pair of shoes, but can't, so just looks back once to the door, then across the room, to the Show, the cereal crunching now in his inner ear, his socked feet crossed on the coffee table.

Every night should be like this, he thinks. A *good* night.

He smiles, covers it with his cereal hand, and finds himself looking at the front window again, lowering his brow suggestively, comparing it and the television screen. One is color, though, the other washed out black and white. But maybe there are more colors, right? More than just red and green and whatever that third one is . . . *indigo*?

Forget it.

He draws the curtains in his mind, sparing himself the indignity or rising to actually do it, as if he were scared, and then makes himself look back to the Show. It's just now starting—he's just now tilting his head forward, into the camera, asking the audience a question, all his weight already on the balls of his feet, so he can open his body up, step aside, let the Episode *unfold*, only, only—

The actors behind him, they're not in a living room or a laboratory or a spaceship, or scrabbling around in the rubble of a lost world, they're at *Plymouth Rock*. Not in the studio's estimation of Pilgrim garb, either, but in Viking leather, their flatboat bobbing in the shallows behind them.

One of the History Episodes. One of the ones that doesn't make the audience question where they're going, but where they're from. One of the episodes that pulls the figurative carpet out from under their figurative selves.

And the actors, Mr. Rod Serling almost recognizes them, almost remembers them from other shows, side bits in movies, guest appearances, commercials, but can't quite attach a name to them, or anything said out in the parking lot, about cigarettes or weather or life or the Show, even, what an honor it is, etc.

That's not what makes him sit up, though, Mr. Rod Serling. There are lots of names he already can't remember. What makes him sit up, lowering his feet to the ground, his cereal spilling into the cushions, forgotten, buried in the ash of a thousand cigarettes, is the question he's asking at least five years ago: *What if somebody got there* before *Columbus*?

The emphasis on 'before,' too, it's perfect, just how Mr. Rod

Serling would have said it, if he'd ever said it, but the thing is, he never had.

This episode had never been written, shot, aired, *thought* of.

Yet there he was, leading the audience into it.

On his couch, Mr. Rod Serling leans forward, across the coffee table, to touch the screen, but then, at the last instant, doesn't.

During the commercial break, Rod Serling watches the rest of the episode then walks upstairs as if through a fog, sits on his bed in his slippers with his eyes narrowed at the floor, trying to remember having ever said those words.

Ten minutes later, he says them aloud as best he can recall them, and hits 'before' just the same, but can no longer tease apart influence and memory—whether he's saying it like that because he just heard himself say it like that, or if he's saying it like that because he practiced it in his office one morning, looking into a hand mirror held down in the deep drawer he was supposed to keep files in.

He doesn't even know the name of the episode—*1492?*—or its season.

And then the commercial break is over and it's morning, and he's driving to the studio, pulling up to the gate. The security guard recognizes him of course, acts scared like he presumably always used to, then holds Mr. Rod Serling up longer than Mr. Rod Serling really wants to be held up, only delivering his one important line as Mr. Rod Serling is pulling away: "You barely missed him."

The clutch goes back in; the car rolls back, the brake lights flaring.

"Mr. Albright," the security guard flashes, like a question. When Mr. Rod Serling doesn't disagree, the security guard explains how Mr. Albright was shooting all night, just left ten minutes ago.

Mr. Rod Serling jots down the address the guard gives him and goes there, and by the size of the house it's obvious Mr. Albright is a director, a producer—that, in all likelihood, the Show was what made him too. Meaning they should have that to share.

"Rod Rod Rod," Mr. Albright says, at the door, stepping aside, and Mr. Rod Serling walks in, taking his sunglasses off just as he steps over the threshold, a private superstition, but, all the same, one that's never let him down.

The conversation starts out casual, just talk about the old days—how many takes it took to get that little girl to quit crying that time, how the star they brought in had to be fed each line, word by word—but then Mr. Rod Serling leans back into the chair he's in, both hands holding the armrests.

Mr. Albright's wearing a kimono and sunglasses, of course. Drink in hand.

Mr. Rod Serling asks him if he saw the Episode last night, and Mr. Albright says—in his shrugging, distracted way—"Not last night, no."

It's funny, true, maybe even clever, and more importantly, it gives Mr. Rod Serling a chance to smile like none of this matters. The cuticles around his fingernails are bone white, though. He shrugs as if just compelled to finish the query, now, says it was that one about the Indians, he guesses, and when Mr. Albright tips his head back, spanning the distance between his chin and nose with the thumb and forefinger of one hand, Mr. Rod Serling sketches it for him: the one where the Indian's chasing a deer through the woods, missing it with arrow after arrow, until he's lost, bursting out of the woods onto a beach. Only there's Vikings there, tasting the sand. The Indian and the

Vikings lock eyes, and, after a great chase, the Vikings haul the Indian onto their flatboat, where a Franciscan priest—"Bede?" Mr. Rod Serling suggests—where a Franciscan priest with absolute *marbles* for eyes tells the Indian—"

"In English, he says this?" Mr. Albright interrupts.

Yes. In *English* this priest tells the Indian of these white skins in their boats, and then, as a parting gift, the Vikings give the Indian a primitive black powder gun, the barrel scrimshawed with Chinese ideograms, and tells him there, there, on the beach, stand guard, shoot the first white man that steps out of his boat, and the Indian nods, his mouth in a frown already, and then stands there for hours and hours with the gun he knows how to use now, until he's still enough that the deer he was chasing steps lightly out onto the sand.

The Indian smiles, lowers his gun, and—Mr. Rod Serling is watching Mr. Albright now, for a flicker of recognition—says that that's when he, Mr. Rod Serling steps in, the gun going off well behind him, to keep the censors happy. But we all know what the Indian chose to shoot: dinner.

"Beautiful," Mr. Albright says.

"I know," Mr. Rod Serling says back. "What season was that, though?"

"You don't remember?"

"That was when I was dating that—"

Mr. Albright smiles, nods, doesn't make him finish.

"Maybe the third," he says.

"But you remember it?"

He looks down to Mr. Rod Serling, then.

"You *wrote* it, didn't you?"

Nod, nod, yes. Of course.

In his car minutes later, half an hour late for a fake lunch, Mr. Rod Serling looks back to Mr. Albright's front door and sees, in the glass around the door, a wash of red silk, a dragon sinuous up one side, the man in it watching.

The tires chirp on accident as he pulls away, and then on purpose at the first intersection, and now Mr. Rod Serling's saying it to himself: *I wrote it. Of course I wrote it.*

Except.

That afternoon, his hair windblown from hours of thinking, Mr. Rod Serling pulls up to the studio gate again. The same security guard steps out, touching the brim of his hat in mock fatigue.

"Find him?" he asks.

Mr. Rod Serling nods, impatient, and says he wants to see the old set if he can, and the guard looks at his watch, winks, and says his shift's over in five, four, three, two . . .

Mr. Rod Serling noses his car into a visitor slot, hugs the walls all the way to the old studio, flinching at everything now, all the old Episodes rising around him, until, by the time he reaches the soundstage, he knows what he's going to find: a working robot of himself. A Serling puppet on piano wire. A rubber mask molded from his face while he slept. An alien fungus he touched on a rail once, that grew into his own likeness. The twin brother he never knew he had, or the cousin he'd always shared clothes with growing up, only now the cousin has had plastic surgery, has had his voice box worked on.

Or, worse, the person he is now is the ghost, the soul that moved on, leaving the body behind after death, a husk, only Mr. Albright and crew reanimated it with ratings or cigarette smoke, put it through the paces.

When he opens the door, Mr. Rod Serling, it's with a certain amount of apprehension.

The soundstage is dark, of course, and being used for something else now, but the general contours are the same, the emotional landscape, and Mr. Rod Serling smiles. Nostalgia. The hole knocked in the wall by some long-ago ladder is still there, even. It was where Merle the janitor used to drop stuff, on accident, when nobody was supposed to be looking, so he could come back for it later. It was also a tip jar, though, of sorts—coins in apology for spilling paint, then walking through it, all over the set. It was where Merle had put the pair of glasses from that first Episode, too, so he could harvest the arms later. Back before anybody knew there was going to be Memorabilia. But those glasses.

Instead of going to Props, to all the cardboard boxes in which he's sure he'll find himself, carved in wood—a skull, Yorick, decaying—he goes to the wall, the hole in the wall, and reaches in as far as he can, until his fingertips touch the glasses he thinks, but then he draws his hand back. He'd bleeding; the glass cut him.

He's Mr. Rod Serling, though. Of course he reaches in again.

After the last commercial break, it's night, and Mr. Rod Serling is a pair of socked feet in the kitchen, pouring dry cereal into another bowl, and the only thing different is that he's wearing those shattered glasses. It makes navigating the kitchen hard, but he does it anyway, holding the bowl in the crook of his arm so he can ease them off his nose the slightest bit as he crosses the threshold from the kitchen to the living room, where he can already hear his voice.

What Episode tonight, right?

He smiles, not able to help already trying to place his monologue, attach it to a title, a season, an actor or actress, but then he stops again, halfway to the couch: the television set is off.

Through the cracked lenses he thinks he sees, for an impossible instant, the Indian from last night's episode, standing with his Chinese gun and his Franciscan advice, all of America behind him, but then the figure is too dark. And doesn't have a face.

Mr. Rod Serling drops his cereal. It arranges itself in a meaningful design around his feet, some of the flakes falling so far as the couch, even.

He is an alien, a clone, a robot, a puppet, a dead man.

And the Vikings, they were *real* Vikings.

He shakes his head no, please, that this is *not* a good night. Not at all.

Through the fractured glasses he can see the figure standing facing the open door has no face, and, worse, is there in total disregard.

But no. It's not that he has no face, it's that he has his back to the room. And he's talking to somebody, through a camera, just there past the open door, recording all this, and it's only then that Mr. Rod Serling looks to the man's feet, his leather shoes.

It's not so much what they're made of that causes Mr. Rod Serling to start screaming, pleading, it's the way the man is standing in them, with none of the weight on the blocky heels, so that, on cue, he can swivel to the side like a showman, sweeping his arm out to include all of this—not a dimension of sight or sound, but of mind.

A great man once wondered if he wasn't just a butterfly dreaming he was a man. But perhaps it's not like that. Perhaps butterflies simply dream of other butterflies. Of smaller and smaller butterflies.

Accept please the example of Mr. Rod Serling, dreamer, citizen of a place he knows all too well.

DEATHTRAP WHIRLPOOL

So I'm standing at the third of eight urinals kind of just spacing out, not breathing too deep, not making any face like I'm over-enjoying myself here, eyes straight-straight ahead, when a guy's chin is suddenly on my shoulder, his whiskers rasping against the fabric of my jacket, his voice tunneling down my ear, roller-coastering into my head, splashing behind my eyes: *"This is the only place we can talk, man."*

I flinch forward, remember there's only the slick pee of a thousand strangers to fall into, so then have to lean back. Into the chest of my new worst friend.

My hands are occupied, too, of course, so I can't even really push him off without making a mess of myself.

I've always half-feared getting stabbed in the kidney while peeing, or maybe kicked in the back of the head.

Not whispered to. Not told a secret.

It's worse, somehow. More intimate.

And of course we're all alone in here. There's no one for me to appeal to with a look. Nobody who can confirm the obvious lunacy of this situation.

All I can do, finally, is step over to the next urinal, kind of drawing a wet line on the tile wall between.

"Yeah, yeah, forgot," the guy says, stepping up to my urinal and unzipping far too loudly. "Appearances."

What I don't do here is look over at him.

Also, what I can't help but do is sneak a glance.

He could be anybody. He is anybody. Another version of me, even: just a dude off the street. Regular everyday normal clothes. No crazy beard. Eyes not particularly strained. No easy facial tics to recognize his kind by. No scars from past encounters in less forgiving bathrooms.

But still.

I wrap things up, hunch my shoulders to zip and turn away earlier than usual, to make my big getaway.

I should have waited to hear him start, though. That would have been a liquid tether, keeping him there.

He was just standing there for appearances, though.

Before I can get to the double sink, his hand is on my shoulder, his eyes boring into mine.

"Whoah, whoah," I say, smiling just enough so he maybe won't take offense but not enough that he'll get any ideas.

"Hands, right," he says, pushing his sleeves up for the sink. Which is precisely where I could have left. Precisely where I *should* left.

Except he made me backsplash some onto my fingers.

So. We stand there with different waters running.

I shake my head and smile into my sink, already trying to compartmentalize this whole scene up, to tell Molly about later.

"You can feel them out there too, can't you?" he says, talking down into his own sink so that, to anybody behind us—still no one—we'll be strangers, he'll be talking to himself, just another crazy mutterer in a city of them.

"Yep," I tell him. Not without hesitation, but because, of the two options—three, counting no reply at all, I guess, but that's already failed me—it seems the one less likely to send him into some big explanation, the story of his life, his theories about the universe, why he likes skim milk more than abstract paintings of flowers, that whole deathtrap whirlpool.

But of course it happens anyway.

"I'm not saying I'm from the future or anything," he says, the white foam swelling and crackling in his hands, his voice low again like I'm in his confidence. His eyes kind of wowing out to show what he thinks of those other people always claiming to be from 2099 or 4212.

"Me neither," I say, measuring my words more carefully now, my water already uncomfortably hot. My clothes suddenly too tight as well. This men's room just way too small, way too buried, way too remote.

"They've still got television shows, though," he says, definitely thrilled with his discovery.

"Television," I parrot, a countdown already going in my head: my launch sequence. How long until I'm back on the street, not in this guy's particular sphere of crazy.

"It's even bigger then," he says. "Like, everybody's *glued* to it, man. Night and day. I mean, all the big problems, hungers, war, disease, oil, math, that's all been solved by then. Like, generations ago. Seriously."

I catch on *math* but don't say anything.

"Not saying it still looks the same, either, but, you know. It's the same dynamic. People sitting around in their own personal luxury, tuning in to a broadcast. The technology involved would melt our primitive brains, of course, would revolutionize our world—or, I guess it did, it revolutionized our world into theirs. But you get what I'm saying."

"TV."

"Exactly. I knew you could tell. The way you were watching this door, how you kind of snuck up on it, then darted in before their cameras could pick you up. I thought you were a shoplifter, at first. But then I recognized myself in you. You *have* to sneak in, right? If you make an announcement of it, everybody in the future, on their couches, they all get ready to place their bets."

I swallow just to stall, I think, and try to think back to my approach.

At one time I *was* a shoplifter, that's the thing. Maybe old habits, lurky old ways of moving, they don't go away unless you make them go away?

"Listen, I've got to—" I start.

"You think that when you choose X or Y," he goes on, oblivious, "that when you go down this hall or that other one, when they both lead to the same place, are the same length—I know that doesn't make sense, but go with me—you think that's all your decision. But their shows, man. How they work. It's genius. And, understand that they're past money, of course. Their currency, how they gauge social status, it's all about influence. That's the big thing then. There."

"Influence."

"And, I'm not just supersure of the tech for this, but I think it's probably like microphones. What they do is they choose hall X or hall Y for you, right? Just, arbitrarily, complete guesswork, or maybe they've been watching you, think they know your habits, can really predict. But then they try to make it come *true*. By yelling into their little microphones, louder and louder, like really ragging their throats out, going for blood, who cares about tomorrow, *that* kind of yelling. That voice you hear in the back of your head, telling you no no no no? That's them, man. That's thousands of them reaching back through time, that's millions of them all chanting together, all desperate for you to go this way instead of that way. When *neither* way really matters at all. But that's all they've got anymore, right? That's all they've got left to do."

I rattle my paper towel from the dispenser, bunch it between my hands.

"It's like that," he goes on, pinching the words from the air, "it's like that magic kind of thinking you had when you were a kid, where you just know that if you twist that doorknob a second time, then that's making some kind of secret difference. But it *does*, see? To them. It's like we're puppets. Like the past is a play to them. One they can't keep their fingers out of."

"But bathrooms," I say, balling my paper towel up, arcing it into the black hole between the sinks.

He does the same, like that makes us brothers, comrades, fellow prisoners.

"*Censors,*" he says, flashing his eyes all around the empty men's room.

I take another paper towel. Just because I don't know what to do with my hands anymore.

He takes one too.

"Censors, decency," he says, too close to me again. "They can follow you shopping, at work, in transit, at home, at family reunions—wherever there's decisions to be made. But, when you picked that third urinal, it was all you, wasn't it? You didn't hear any voices trying to get you to go all the way to the end, right? Of course you didn't. Their cameras, they can't look into our bathrooms, man. Because this is *network* for them. It's supposed to be safe for the kiddies, the grandmas. Something you can watch while eating dinner."

Just to keep him from seeing my eyes—it makes sense, a show not going into the bathroom with the character—I track over to that third urinal.

It's still there. Waiting for me. Calling to me.

"So this is the only place we're really *us* anymore, man," he says, so earnest now. So desperate for me to see what he's saying. Then he's even quieter for the next part: "*The only time they're not in our heads, controlling us.*"

I bite my lip in, nod in what I hope's not a superior way.

We're finally to the tinfoil helmet part of the afternoon.

"Um," I say, palming my wallet like an apology, "I got a dollar, I guess."

He looks down to my hand then tracks back up to my face, these sad parentheses around his eyes, his lips somehow shaped like the worst question mark.

"They're *out* there, man," he says. "You're a star in their world, don't you see? We all are. Every little moment of the day. Every turn, every decision, every choice. Their whole world hangs on it. You can feel it, right? Hear it? Kind of—?" and he touches the back of his head, to show.

I leave him standing there, marooned in the men's room for however long this episode is going to last. I try to wish some good meds back to him, or for a sister or a dad to find him, reel him back in. But it's not going to be me. Sorry, bub. Wrong dude, wrong bathroom. I walk out not really smiling, but definitely relieved, my hands clean, the day bright, my dollar back in my wallet, my bladder sagging in on itself so that I have to picture it like a raisin, spent.

Only.

The first obstacle I have to step around is just a normal, beat-up table.

I fake left, go right at the last moment.

Next is a woman a blue pantsuit, her heels clacky.

We dance left, we dance right, and finally she smiles and commits to her left, leaving me to go to my left, completely randomly, the two us grinning to each other about the stupid complexity of it all. Just the simple mechanics of navigating a sidewalk.

After her is a planter seeded with cigarette butts.

To show I'm my own person, I step up onto its front ledge, take neither the X way around nor the Y way, but, when I come down all true Z, my hands still pocketed, my face ready to be pleasant, my whole body leaning into the future, I feel something like a sigh in the back my head. Like one person out of a hundred million made a longshot pie-in-the-sky gamble that just came true. Like all their whispers into their microphone finally made it through. To me. Here.

I keep my hands in my pockets but am pushing them in deeper now. I breathe in, trying to fill this new hollowness in my chest.

If I looked back, would the guy be watching me from the doorway of the bathroom?

If I looked back, would a cigarette tree be unfurling itself from the planter, in celebration?

Yes. No. Maybe.

I purse my lips, swallow the smile I don't really mean.

Dear Molly, I say in my head, wincing. *I think we're live.*

ZOMBIE SHARKS WITH METAL TEETH

It's supposed to be like killing a mouse, killing this mouse, that's what Ronald said, but it isn't.

"Ronald," I say, trying to make my voice loop over my shoulder to him.

He's in his chair by the specimen refrigerator.

"Just do it," he says.

"He's looking at me, though."

Ronald's chair scrapes, air hisses through his teeth, and then he's there, with me.

"You're supposed to be a research *assistant*," he says, taking the mouse from me, the syringe riding from its back like a tranquilizer dart, "not a *trainee*."

The mouse. I was thinking about naming him Mr. Cheese. Or Danger Bob, from his trick with the wheel.

Ronald slams the plunger down and it doesn't even have to be sodium pentathol. There's enough of it that it could be water, or even more blood: it floods Danger Bob's internal organs, stretches his skin taut so that it's pink under his white hair, like an old man going bald.

Sodium pentathol isn't really standard for mice, but neither's what Ronald had been doing to it for the last week.

He holds it up to his face, watches it die, and I think maybe Danger Bob is going to whisper something to him finally, some secret of biology, of rodent psychology, but then, instead, all we get is a drop of sodium pentathol seeping out Danger Bob's right nostril, spidering down to the end of a whisker.

Ronald drops the mouse cadaver—his term, like with everything—into the red biohazard bag and looks around the lab for the next great experiment, his eyes narrowing on each station, each cage, each device.

I hate my job.

In the supply room after work I mouth a silent prayer for Danger Bob, and nod again like I'm watching his trick on the wheel.

The next morning Ronald gets to the lab before me, leaves the door chocked open. I walk in slow, trying to see everything all at once, and Ronald's in his chair by the fridge, watching me.

"Good morning," he says.

I shrug, tell him to tell me, please.

He's already smiling.

It's Danger Bob, back from the afterlife.

I take a long step back.

"He was sleeping by the door to his cage," Ronald says.

"This isn't Bob," I say.

"Ask him."

I watch his eyes after this, not sure I heard right.

"Ask Bob?"

Ronald nods.

"You could have just painted that on his back," I say.

Ronald agrees.

"Ask him," he says again.

I don't want to but I do.

"Louder," Ronald says, like it should be obvious.

"Are you Danger Bob?" I say, again, and it's only because I've been here for four months now that I notice Ronald's right hand is behind his back. His trigger finger. The vein in his neck rises with the tendons in his bicep when the mouse who isn't Danger Bob shakes his head no, and Ronald can't help laughing now.

There's a little white-furred, radio-controlled servo collar around Imposter Bob's neck, its copper leads wired into the neck musculature. So he can shake his head no.

"Quit fucking around," Ronald says, still smiling. "I've got something new for us today."

Some days I'm not sure who's the lab mouse.

The project Ronald was working on when he hired me involved applied telekinesis. What we would do is anesthetize gophers and moles and whatever else we could buy, sever their spinal cords up near their brain stems, then try to condition them to use their own bodies as puppets, lurch across the stainless steel exam table.

The servo collars were what Ronald had to finally use when the financial backers sent their people to check on their investments. It was then that Ronald told me the secret of funding: never do enough to make money, just do enough to get people to give you more.

He thinks when I empty the red biohazard bag, I empty it into the small green medical waste dumpster in the parking lot. But I don't. Instead I fill my pockets with dead rodents then go up onto the roof during break, lay the limp bodies in the white gravel. The hawks scream with delight, fall all around me, and take the moles and gophers and rabbits away. For the mice, because they're white, I have to push all the white gravel away, frame them against the tar. I tried standing them up with toothpicks at first, for dignity, but finally had to just lay them on their sides, their forelegs curled up against their chests.

We're going to hell, of course, me and Ronald. Not just for the animals we kill with truth serum and electricity and surgery, but for the birds that fall sick from the sky into the lives of ordinary people, far, far away, wherever they are.

What Ronald has for us today that's new is beyond telekinesis, beyond Danger Bob's faux-prehensile tail.

I watch him and listen and feel my face making expressions of doubt, then curiosity, then think of a green butterfly for a while, because now he's practicing his pitch on me. Everything bullet points, something Edison would have thought of if he'd had access to the formative experiences of Ronald's childhood.

Or if he'd hated mice.

The green butterfly is an angel, of course. She has the face of a girl I knew in high school.

I nod for Ronald, and for her.

What we're doing today is removing a late-stage mouse fetus from its mother then immersing it in the oxygen rich solution left over from the experiment with the two squirrels. Immersing it in there so it can breathe.

"Nutrients?" Ronald asks, as if I'd said it.

I nod, as if I'd just been about to say it, yes.

"They're in there," he says, dismissing my lack of education, staring at me to be sure I get the point.

"Sorry," I say. "Go on."

He smiles, does.

After the mouse—I'm already calling him Zipper Boy—after the mouse is successfully transferred to his glass womb, the fish tank the squirrels had died in, too stubborn to evolve gills, after the mouse is in there, that's when the real science begins: his arms in the long rubber gloves, Ronald will remove Zipper Boy's cartilage skull, exposing the still-developing brain.

He touches the side of his own head to be sure I'm following, not picturing myself on the roof, holding Zipper Boy up in my palm, eyes cast down, a great, moist shadow darkening around me, the underside of her wings iridescent.

I touch my own head back, right in the temple, and Ronald stares at me, looks away.

"The *folds*," he says, "it's the basic mammalian *characteristic*, right? Why are they there, though?"

"So the brain can fit," I say back.

He nods, smiles, says it again: "So the brain can fit. Because, if it didn't fold, then the mother's pelvis would break and there would be no rearing of the young, and it wouldn't matter *how* smart we were, *how* many tools we could *eventually* make."

I tell him okay.

He shrugs, like I'm challenging him. "So what do you think we could accomplish without that limitation?" he says, low, still paranoid that the bats that were delivered by accident are actually industrial spies.

I'm supposed to be catching them, but keep not doing it.

"Anything?" I say.

He nods.

"Anything," he says back, and then for the rest of the morning I have to hold the suction tube to Zipper Boy's head while Ronald performs minor surgery. I'm supposed to catch the blood, keep the water clear, cycle in more.

"Scuba Mouse," Ronald says, through his mask.

I shake my head no.

Two weeks later, Zipper Boy's brain blooms open in the tank like the enhanced pictures you see of distant, exploding galaxies.

I find myself holding my breath each morning in my car, before I walk in. It's not enough.

* * *

By the forty-second day, the investors want to see what they're paying for. I lay on the roof looking over the edge. Their cars pull up just before lunch. The only thing different for them about Ronald is how he's bald now, shaved. The eye solution he uses to hide the red around the rims is his own compound. He offers it to me on a regular basis, and on a regular basis I decline.

I walk down the metal stairs in time to hear his latest pitch for time travel, how of *course* you can't send living tissue through any kind of disintegrating field then expect it to be reassembled properly on the other end. But *inert* matter, yes. Ronald's solution is typically elegant: the time traveler should simply offer to be killed moments before passing through the field, moments *after* his team has pushed through all the medical equipment and information brochures the people on the other end will need to revive this dead man from the future, or the past.

I see one of the investors holding his chin, nodding, thinking of the tactical uses this could provide, but when he sees the way I'm looking at him he stops, rubs his cheek.

"Don't worry about him," Ronald says about me.

They don't.

Eight minutes later—the same amount of time it takes sunlight to get here—Ronald is demonstrating what they all saw last time: the modified television set he's learned to tune the future in with. One *hour* in the future, anyway. For the area right around the specimen table. He's not showing them the modified set so much, though, as what's on it's screen: the investors, all signing checks. It's really a tape of them from last time.

"Show us why, though," one of them says.

Why they'll sign. Ronald smiles, nods, is already standing amid all the bent silverware before Zipper Boy's tank, waiting for them to see it.

"Like he's a *god?*" one of the investors says, looking around for support. Like Zipper Boy's a god is what he's saying. One we bring offerings to.

Ronald shushes him, his teeth together.

"I don't think so . . ." another investor says, staring hard at Ronald, as if reading his eyes. "You didn't leave this for him did you, son?"

Ronald shakes his head no, his dimples sucking into a smile he's trying hard to swallow.

"No *way,*" the third and final investor says.

Ronald shrugs, is a carnival barker now, holding his hand out for the third investor's stainless steel, monogrammed pen.

Zipper Boy bends it into a nearly perfect circle with his unfolded mind, then, bored with it, allows it to clatter to the ground.

The milky surface of his water bubbles.

He could live forever in there.

The girlfriend I choose, because I want this all to be over but for it not to be my fault, she's ASPCA. Militant, probably a vegetarian even. I wear leather to get her to introduce herself, then lure her to my car, to lunch, a series of dinners and movies and phone calls, until one day, not on accident, I leave an expired rodent in my right hand pocket, plan to pull it out to open my car door with, only notice it's a mouse when its nose won't fit into the keyhole.

The movie we see that night is about a submarine family chosen, for obvious reasons, to be astronauts. Which is all good and fine until the mother has her third child, her first in space.

The amniotic fluid floats through the space station and into the ventilation system, then, with the help of alien spores or cosmic rays—a movie device—transforms the whole station into a womb in which the family gestates, emerging nine months later to look down on earth's blue sphere, and cry, the vacuum of space wicking their tears away. Finally, the firstborn son flares the new membrane around his neck out and it catches the solar wind and the family holds hands, retreats into the outer reaches of the solar system, still together.

My girlfriend—Mandy, I think, if I heard right—cries with the aliens, holds my hand, and I hold onto the armrest.

Afterwards, by the water fountains, I try to tell her about Ronald but fail, just lead her out to the parking lot for my charade, which fails too when I open my pocket and, instead of a dead mouse, pale green butterflies flutter up around us.

Mandy starts to catch one but I stop her, and my hand firm around her wrist is the beginning of the end for us: that I would deny her that.

The next morning Ronald asks me how my experiment went?

I'm tapping vitamins into Zipper Boy's tank when he asks it, and I'm not sure if his lips move, or if they move with the words he's saying.

On the surface of the water, dead, is a pale green butterfly.

Love is a spoon, Zipper Boy says to me in my head.

Across the room, Ronald waits for me to answer, to agree.

Zipper Boy's brain is seventeen times the size of his body now.

We're not sure what he can do if he really wants to.

The thing I notice about the silverware on the ground that afternoon is that it's real silver. Which should be less of a challenge, really. An insult. Another thing is that it's straight, all of it. I bend down to it, know instantly without wanting to that this is Ronald's mother's mother's silverware. And that the only reason it would be straight, now, on the ground, is that Ronald brought it to Zipper Boy bent.

Across the lab, Ronald is hunched over the circuit board of the echolocation device he's retroengineering from the dolphin head he had delivered in a cooler of ice. It cost four thousand dollars, is supposed to locate the bats for us somehow. When I opened the cooler, the dolphin was smiling. But maybe that's all they know how to do.

I don't care about the bats, really.

But the silverware. The swimming goggles Ronald's wearing now, each lens sloshing with his compound.

Love is love, Zipper Boy says in my head, like he's finishing an argument.

Without looking at his tank I think back that he was never even *born*.

The surface of his water undulates with thought, and either he speaks back to me through Ronald or Ronald speaks back himself: "A mother's love for her unborn young is the purest love there is," he says. "Because it hasn't yet fallen victim to the large eyes of infancy."

I sweep up the bat guano until noon then climb the stairs to the roof.

Danger Bob is waiting for me. I cry into my hands, think maybe the whole world can see me up there.

"It's okay," Danger Bob says from behind his three-inch exhaust pipe, and to show, he scurries furiously across the white gravel, invisible until the last moment when his small body is about to silhouette itself against the low, brick-red retaining wall.

I see whiskers, the shadow of an ear, then look away.

In my pocket now is all of Ronald's mother's mother's silverware. I don't know what to do with it.

Two days later I find the first draft of the article Ronald's writing for the neuromags. In it, Zipper Boy is Scuba Mouse, and I've been betrayed.

Beside me, too, I can feel Zipper Boy watching me.

It's something Ronald's tracked in his article—how his Scuba Mouse is now discovering his body, learning to use it, look through it. In a footnote, Ronald sketches out the helmet he's going to build his Scuba Mouse. It's filled with water, a failed diving bell. There will be no leash, either, no air hose, no tether. Just a mouse, teetering out into the world, wholly unaware what love is, even.

Already all the other caged rodents in the lab are dead, overflowing from the red biohazard container.

Ronald says Zipper Boy tells him it's not murder, because they were never really *alive*.

He's the one talking to a mouse now. I don't tell that to him, just shrug, look away, at a bat crawling nose first down the wall, stalking a cricket.

Ronald throws the dolphin head at it, misses.

My hand is shaking from something—from *this*.

When Ronald collects his precious dolphin head he finds the cricket lodged in the basal ganglia and stares at it for an unhealthy period of time. Embarrassed, I look away. Zipper Boy's water is 92 degrees Fahrenheit. The phone rings fourteen times, and fourteen times, we don't answer it.

When the human race ends, this is the way it will happen, I know.

That night I kidnap Mandy a little bit then sit with her—bound hand and foot in the trunk of my car—and watch the city bats coalesce above the three-inch exhaust pipe of the lab. Insects are swirling up out of it, clockwise, and I smile, rename the insects *manna bug, moses beetle*, and realize I can't take Mandy into this place. That I either love her too much or I could love her too much, which, really, is the same thing.

I inject her with a non-lethal dose of sodium pentathol and lead her into her building, careful not to ask her any questions, even in a disguised voice. Her doorman takes her without question, nods to me once, and I fade back into the night.

The green butterfly from the girl in high school was the one I found on her windshield one day at lunch, when I'd finally got my nerve up to wait for her, say something.

From across town Zipper Boy says into my head, in her voice, *Hungry there?* and I sulk away, my hands in my pockets.

Love isn't a spoon, I say back to him from the parking lot, the next morning, and this time when I walk in Ronald has the dolphin head on a long, metal stick.

"Scarecrow," he says, about it, then explains in his most offhand voice how bats are really just mice with wings, meaning the mouse part of their brains must still remember the long winters spent under the snow, walking lightly, because the coyotes were up there somewhere, listening, listening, finally slinking off to the water's edge, for clam, then fish, then they keep going out deeper and deeper, testing their lungs, until they're dolphins. "Look at the teeth," he says, running his finger along the dolphin's jaw line.

I close my eyes to think.

"They—they weren't coyotes then, though," I say, pinching the bridge of my nose between the thumb and forefinger of my right hand.

"Doesn't matter," Ronald says. "They didn't know they were mice then either, right?"

He stares at me until I nod, hook my chin to the tank.

"You fed him already?"

He shrugs—maybe, maybe not. This is kindergarten. The new title of his article on Zipper Boy is "Tidings from the Tidal Pool." Even I know it won't translate well—that, being a scientific article, it *needs* to—but before I can tell him, something pops above our heads.

Ronald doesn't look up from his paper. I have to.

"Security," he says.

It's a row of cameras, motion activated. *Bat*-activated.

"What?" I ask.

Ronald shrugs. "Scuby here says their REM patterns are—unusual for rodents. Like how when a dog dreams about chasing a car, its leg will kick?"

"Maybe it's having a karate dream."

"Whatever. It's a luxury bats don't have, right? One kick, they're falling . . ." He shrugs again, already bored with this. ". . . think it has something to do with circulation to their brain. Probably need to get an opossum in here to see, though—upside down, all that. It's a marsupial, though, I don't know . . ."

"I'm not doing it," I tell him.

"What?"

"Sleeping upside down."

"I'm not asking."

"Okay."

"Well."

"Yeah."

I work at my table counting salmon eggs into vials, careful to keep my back to the leering dolphin.

Love isn't a spoon, I know. It's got to be something, though.

That night while I'm gone, Ronald somehow manages to spray the dolphin head with liquid nitrogen, to keep it from rotting.

Over lunch, from his office, I call Mandy's work number to report a crime but she doesn't answer. I hang up, hold the phone there for what I know is too long.

Through the plate glass of Ronald's open-air cubicle, Zipper Boy watches me, manages to rewind my memory to the movie about the submarine family then play it again, without the zero-g amniotic fluid. This time, the birth is achieved through a primitive but functional teleportation device: one moment, the baby isn't there, and the next it is, the mother's stomach already deflating, the father guiding it back down like deflating a raft.

I shake my head no, don't want to see anymore, but Zipper Boy forces it on me, in me, and I have to watch this infant grow into an adolescent who appears normal until we follow him into his cabin. There, he reads books on what appropriate emotional reactions are to certain social stimuli, then, as a young man, standing over the father he's just slain, we understand that the reason he is the way he is is that he was denied the essential violence of birth. That his whole life he's been searching for that.

It's Zipper Boy's story. He's never been born either.

I'm sorry, I think to him, but it's too late, he's dreaming with the bats again, flitting with them through their night made of sound, his small, atrophied feet perfectly still.

I envy him, a little. But the rest of me knows what's happening.

The mechanism I'm reduced to is ridiculously simple, as most are: I simply take Ronald's mother's mother's silverware down to the pawn shop, get a ticket for it, then leave it on the bulletin board.

Ronald sees it first thing after lunch, stares at it, and walks away, then comes back again and again, until he looks across the room to me.

"You do this?" he says.

"We needed supplies," I tell him.

Zipper Boy's water gurgles. Ronald looks from it to me.

"*Supplies?*" he says.

"Guess the lab fairy skipped us this month," I say back.

Ronald smiles; it's what he told me my first week here, when I forgot to pick up everything he'd ordered—that the *lab fairy* wasn't going to bring it, was she?

I have no idea what Zipper Boy is telling him.

Ronald shrugs, stands, looking in the direction of the pawn shop already.

"It wasn't really as great as you thought it was," he says, in parting. "Number four's trick."

Danger Bob, on his wheel.

My right hand wraps itself into a fist and I have to look away, swallow hard. Science isn't cold. Not even close.

Ronald laughs on his way out, trailing his fingers over his shoulder.

"Stay off the roof, too," he calls back. "I think it's shaking the cameras."

I stare at him until he's gone then track up to the cameras. Because there's no way in a world of brick and stone that my footsteps could come through the ceiling. But Ronald was just saying that, I see now; what he wanted me to see was that each camera is on one of the old, radio-controlled servos. That he still has the trigger out in the parking lot. That the guidewires their board is hanging from are the perfect antenna. That he's going to be documenting whatever I wanted him out of the lab for.

Zipper Boy smiles, with his real mouth. His teeth dull from disuse. From never-use.

But his mind.

I take a step towards his tank and the room fills with pale green butterflies, the dust on their wings graphite-fine, and

I have to breathe it, can hear the cameras snapping me in sequence, one after another, down the board, and the butterflies start to fill me. Light-headed.

But no.

Like the girl from high school said, *meant*, I take the first one I can catch, take it between my teeth, and swallow, and then the next, and the next, until they're all gone, and I say it to Zipper Boy. That every experiment needs a control. Someone to exercise it. That I understand that now.

He's just staring at me now.

Love, he says in my head.

You understand, I say back. *That's why I'm doing this. Please.*

In his water, for me, Zipper Boy tries to do Danger Bob's trick with the wheel, to save himself, but he's not a mouse anymore, and there's no wheel anyway, and it's too late in the game for gymnastics to save us from what we're doing here.

The tears he cries for himself are bubbles of carbon dioxide—spent breath, his infant lungs still new, uncoordinated. The bubbles seep from the corner of his eye, collect on the surface of his water, and he nods, looks away to make this easy on me, but it's not.

Through the cameras, in what will be time-capture, Ronald is watching me, a future Ronald, an hour-from-now Ronald, and I'm sitting by him, trying to explain, to keep my job.

Listen, Zipper Boy says. It's a kindness and I do, and the-me-from-then knows, has it right: what I have to do now is what I can feel myself already doing—move my arms from the wrist, my legs from the foot, my head from the chin, so that, on film, when I take the salt shaker, empty it into the tank, it will look like suicide. Like Zipper Boy had made me his puppet. Chose me instead of Ronald because I was weaker.

It's a thing Ronald could buy. That he would buy.

But then, without meaning too—scientific curiosity, the reason I responded to Ronald's ad in the first place, maybe—I look too long, another hour into the future, past him accepting my explanation for homicide, to the way he stands up from his chair smiling, holding one of the early bat-dream negatives up to the light, so that the colors are reversed. This is one of the images from the camera on the end of the board, which was aimed wrong. Instead of the bats, it had been snapping pictures of the dolphin head, only—looking along his arm I can see it in the modified television set—the dolphin's teeth in the reverse-color image are silver, silver nitrate, *metal*, and from the angle the camera was at the dolphin isn't even a dolphin anymore, but a predator that can never die, not if Ronald builds it right, this time. Not if it keeps moving.

ROCKET MAN

The dead aren't exactly known for their baseball skills, but still, if you're a player short some afternoon, just need a body to prop up out in left field—it all comes down to how bad you want to play, really. Or, in our case—where you can understand that by 'our' I mean 'my,' in that I promised off four of my dad's cigarettes, one of my big brother's magazines, and one sleepover lie—how bad you want to impress Amber Watson, on the walk back from the community pool, her lifeguard eyes already focused on everything at once.

Last week, I'd actually smacked the ball so hard that Rory at shortstop called time, to show how the cover'd rolled half back, the red stitching popped.

"You scalped it," he said, kind of curling his lip in awe.

I should mention I'm Indian, except everybody's always doing that for me.

The plan that day we pulled a zombie in (it had used to be Michael T from over on Oak Circle, but you're not supposed to call zombies by their people names), my plan was to hit that same ball—I'd been saving it—even harder, so that there'd just be a cork center twirling up over our diamond, trailing leather and thread. Amber Watson would track back from that cracking sound to me, still holding my follow-through like I was posing for a trophy. And then of course I'd look through the chain link, kind of nod to her that this was me, yeah, this was who I really am, she's just never seen it, and she'd smile and look away, and things in the halls at school would be different between us then. More awkward. She might even start timing her walks to coincide with some guess at my spot in the batting order.

Anyway, it wasn't like there was anything else I could ever possibly do that might have a chance of impressing her.

But first, of course, we needed that body to prop up out in left field. Which, I know you're thinking 'right, *right* field,' these are sixth graders, they never wait, they always step out, slap the ball early, and, I mean, maybe the kids from Chesterton or Memphis City do, I don't know. But around here, we've been taught to wait, to time it out, to let that ball kind of hover in the pocket before we launch it into orbit. Kids from Chesterton? None of them are ever going pro. Not like us.

It's why we fail the spelling test each Friday, why we blow the math quiz if we're not sitting by somebody smart. You don't need to know how to spell 'homerun' to hit one. You don't have to add up runners in your head, so long as you knock them all in. Easy as that.

As for Michael T, none of us had had much to do with him since he got bit, started playing for the other team. There were the lunges from behind the fence on the way to school, there was that shape kind of scuffling around when you took the trash out some nights, but that could have been any zombie. It didn't have to be Michael T. And, pulling him in that day to just stand there, let the flies buzz in and out of his mouth—it's not like that's not what he did *before* he was dead. You only picked Michael T if he was the only one to pick, I'm saying. You wouldn't think that either, him being a year older than us and all, but he'd always just been our size, too. Most kids like that, a grade up but not taller, they'd at least be fast, or be able to fling the ball home all the way from the center fence. Not Michael T. Michael T—the best way to explain him, I guess, it's that his big brother used to pin him down to the ground at recess, drop a line of spit down almost to his face, the rest of us looking but not looking. Glad just not to be him.

That day, though, with Amber Watson approaching on my radar, barefoot the way she usually was, her shoes hooked over her shoulder like a rich lady's purse, that day, it was either Michael T or nobody. Or, at first it *was* nobody, but then, just joking around, Theodore said he'd seen Michael T shuffling around down by the rocket park anyway.

"Michael *T*?" I asked.

"He still can't catch," Theodore said.

"That was all the way before lunch, though, yeah?" Rory said, socking the ball into his glove for punctuation.

It was nearly three, now.

"Can you track him?" Les said, falling in as we rounded the backstop.

"Your nose not work?" I asked him back.

Just another perfect summer afternoon.

We kicked a lopsided rock nearly all the way to where Michael T was supposed to have been, and then we turned to Theodore. He shrugged, was ready to fight any of us, even tried some of the words he'd learned from spying on his uncles in the garage. He wasn't lying, though. Splatted all over the bench were the crab apples him and Jefferson Banks had been zinging Michael T with.

"Jefferson," I said, "what about him?"

"Said he had to go home," Theodore shrugged, half-embarrassed for Jefferson. "His mom."

Figured. The one time I can impress Amber Watson and Jefferson's cleaning out all the ashtrays in the house then reading romance novels to his mom while she tans in the backyard.

"Who then?" Les asked, shading his eyes from the sun, squinting across all the glinty metal of the old playground.

None of us came to this one anymore. It was for kids.

"He's got to be around," Theodore said. "My dad said they like beef jerky."

I seconded this, had heard it as well.

You could lure a zombie anywhere if you had a twist of dried meat on a long string. It was supposed to be getting bad enough with the high schoolers that the stores in town had put a limit on beef jerky, two per customer.

I kicked at another rock that was there by the bench. It wasn't our lopsided one, was probably one Jefferson and Theodore had tried on Michael T. There was still a little bit of blood on it. All the ants were loving the crab apple leftovers, but, for them, there was a force field around where that rock had been. Until the next rain, anyway.

"She's never going to see me," I said, just out loud.

"Who?" Theodore asked, studying the park like Amber Watson could possibly be walking through it.

I shook my head no, never mind, and, turning away, half-planning to set a mirror up in right field, let Gerald just stand kind of by it, so it would seem like we had a full team, I caught a flash of cloth all the way in the top of the rocket.

"It's not over yet," I said, pointing up there with my chin.

Somebody was up there, right at the top where the astronauts would sit if it were a real rocket. The capsule part. And they were moving.

"Jefferson?" Theodore asked, looking to us for support.

Like monkeys, Les and Rory crawled up the outside of the rocket, high enough that their moms had to be having heart attacks in their kitchens.

When they get there, Rory had to turn to the side to throw up. It took that loogey of puke forever to make it to the ground. We laughed because it was throw-up, then tracked back up to the top of the rocket.

"It's Michael T!" Les called down, waving his hand like there was anywhere else in the whole world we might be looking.

"What's he doing?" I asked, not really loud enough, my eyes kind of pre-squinted, because this might be going to mess our game up.

"It's Jefferson," Theodore filled in, standing right beside me, and he was right.

Instead of going home like his mom wanted, Jefferson had spiraled up into the top of the rocket, probably to check if his name was still there, and never guessed Michael T might still be lurking around. Even a first grader can outrun or outsmart a zombie, but, in a tight place like that, and especially if you're in a panic, are freaking out, then it's a different kind of game altogether.

"Shouldn't have thrown those horse apples at him," Gerald said, shaking his head.

"Shouldn't have been stupid, more like," I said, and slapped my glove into Gerald's chest, for him to hold.

Ten minutes later, Les and Rory using cigarettes from the outside of the rocket to herd him away from his meal, Johnny T lumbered down onto the playground, stood in that crooked, hurt way zombies do.

"Hunh," Theodore said.

He was right.

In the year since Johnny T had been bitten, he hadn't grown any. He was shorter than all us now. Rotted away, Jefferson's gore all drooled down his frontside, some bones showing through the back of his hand, but still, that we'd outgrown him this past year. It felt like we'd cheated.

It was exhilarating.

One of us laughed and the rest fell in, and, using a piece of a sandwich Les finally volunteered to open his elbow scab on—we didn't have any beef jerky—we were able to lure Michael T back to the baseball diamond.

After everybody'd crossed the road, I studied up and down it, to be sure Amber Watson hadn't passed yet.

I didn't think so.

Not on an afternoon this perfect.

So then it was the big vote: whose glove was Michael T going to wear, probably try to gnaw on? When I got tired of it all, I just threw mine into his chest, glared all around.

"Warpath, chief," Les said, picking the glove up gingerly, watching Michael T the whole time.

"Scalp *your* dumb ass," I said, and turned around, didn't watch the complicated maneuver of getting the glove on Michael T's left hand, and only casually kept track of the stupid way he kept breaking position. Finally Timmy found a dead squirrel in the weeds, stuffed it into the school backpack that had kind of become part of Michael T's back. The smell kept him in place better than a spike through his foot. He kept kind of spinning around in his zombie way, tasting the air, but he wasn't going anywhere.

And then—this because my whole body was tuned into it, because the whole summer had been pointing at it—the adult swim whistle went off down at the community pool. Or maybe what I was tuned into was the groan from all the swimmers. Either way, this was always when the lifeguards would change chairs, was always when, if somebody was going off-shift, they would go.

"Amber," I said to myself, tossing my ragged, lucky ball to Les then tapping my bat across home plate, waiting for him to wind up.

"Am-*what*?" Theodore asked from behind the catcher's mask his mom insisted on.

I shook my head no, nothing, and, because I was looking down the street, down that tunnel of trees, Les slipped the first pitch by me.

"That one's free," I called out to him, tapping my bat again. Licking my lips.

Les wound up, leaned back, and I stepped up like I was already going to swing. He cued into it, that I was ahead of him here, and it threw him off enough that he flung the ball over Theodore's mitt, rattled the backstop with it.

"That one's free too," he called out to me, and I smiled, took it.

Just wait, I was saying inside, sneaking a look up the road again, and, just like in the movies, the whole afternoon slowed almost to a stop right there.

It was her. I smiled, nodded, my own breath loud in my ears, and slit my eyes back to Les.

He drove one right into the pocket, and if I'd wanted I could have shoveled it over all of their heads, dropped it out past the fence, into no man's land.

Except it was too early.

After it slapped home, I spun out of the box, spit into the dirt, hammered my bat into the fence two times.

And it was definitely her. Shoes over her shoulder, gum going in her mouth, nose still zinced, jean shorts over her one-piece, the whole deal.

I timed it perfect, getting back to the box, was wound up to *launch* this ball just at the point when she'd be closest to me.

So of course Les threw it high.

I could see it coming a mile away, how he'd tried to knuckle it, had lost it on the downsling like he always did, so there was maybe even a little arc to the ball's path. Not that it mattered, it was too high to swing at, but still—now or never, right? This is what all my planning had come down to.

I stepped back, crowding Theodore, who was already leaned forward to catch the ball when it dropped, and I swung at a ball that was higher than my shoulders, a ball my dad would have already been turning away from in disgust, and knew the instant my bat cracked into it that there wasn't going to be any lift, that it was a line drive, an arrow I was shooting out, blind. One I was going to have to run faster than, somehow.

Still, even though I didn't scoop under it like I would have liked, and even though I was making contact with it earlier than I would have wanted, I gave it every last thing I had, gave it everything I'd learned, everything I had to gamble.

And it worked. The cover flapping behind it just like a comet tail, it was a thing of beauty.

Les being Les, of course he bit the dirt to get out of the way, and Gerald and Rory—second and short—nearly hit each other, diving for what they knew was a two-run hit. A ball that wasn't even going to skip grass until—

Until left field, yeah.

Until Michael T.

And, if you're thinking he raised his glove here, that some long-forgotten reflex surfaced in his zombie brain for an instant, then guess again.

Dead or alive, he would have done the same thing: just stood there like the dunce he was.

Only, now, his face was kind of spongy, I guess.

The ball splatted into his left eye socket, sucked into place, stayed there, some kind of dark juice burping from his ears, trickling down along his jaw, the cover of the ball pasted to his cheek.

For a long moment we were all quiet, all holding our breaths—this was like hitting a pigeon with a pop-fly—and then, of everybody, I was the only one to hear Amber Watson stop on the sidewalk, look from the ball back to me, exactly like I'd planned.

I smiled, kind of shrugged, and then Gerald called it in his best umpire voice: "*Out!*"

I turned to him, my face going cold, and everybody in the in-field was kind of shrugging that, yeah, the ball definitely hadn't hit the ground. No need to burn up the baseline.

"But, but," I said, pointing out to Michael T with my bat, to show how obvious it was that that wasn't a catch, that it didn't really count, and then Rory and Theodore and Les all started nodding that Gerald was right. Worse, now the outfield was chanting: "Mi-chael, Mi-cheal, Mi-chael." And then my own dugout fell in, clapping some Indian whoops from their mouth to memorialize what had happened here, today. How I was the only one who could have done it.

But I wasn't out.

Michael T wasn't even a real player, was just a body we'd propped up out there.

I looked back to Amber Watson and could tell she was just waiting to see what I was going to do here, waiting to see what was going to happen.

So I showed her.

I charged the mound, and, when Les sidestepped, holding his hands up and out like a bullfighter, I kept going, bat in hand, held low behind me, Rory and Gerald each giving me room as well, so that by the time I got out to left field I was running.

"You didn't catch it!" I yelled to Michael T, singlehandedly trying to ruin my whole summer, wreck my love life, trash my reputation—'Even a zombie can get him out'—and I swung for the ball a second time.

Instead of driving it off the T his head was supposed to be, I thunked it deeper, into his brain, I think, so that the rest of him kind of spasmed in a brainstemmy way, the bat shivering out of my hands so I had to let it go. And, because I hadn't planned ahead—charging out of the box isn't exactly about thinking everything through, even my dad would cop to this—the follow-through of my swing, it wrapped me up into Michael T's dead arms, and we fell together, me first.

And, like everything else since Les's failed knuckle ball, it took forever to happen. Long enough for me to hear that little lopsided plastic ball rattling in Amber Watson's whistle right before she set her feet and blew it. Long enough for me to see the legs of a single fly, following us down. Long enough for me to hear my chanted name stop in the middle.

This wasn't just a freak thing happening, anymore.

We were stepping over into legend, now.

Because the town was always on alert these days, Amber Watson's whistle was going to line the fence with people in under five minutes, and now everybody on the field and in the dugout, they were going to be witness to this, were each going to have their own better vantage point to tell the story from.

Meaning, instead of me being the star, everybody else would be.

And, Amber Watson.

It hurt to even think about.

We were going to have a special bond, now, sure, but not the kind where I was ever going to get to buy her a spirit ribbon.

Not the kind where she'd ever tell me to quit smoking, because it was bad for me.

If I even got to live that far, I mean. If the yearbook staff wasn't already working my class photo onto the casualties page.

I wasn't there yet, though.

This wasn't the top of a rocket, I mean.

Sure, I was on my back in left field, and Michael T was over me, pinning me down by accident, the slobber and blood and brain juice stringing down from his lips, swinging right in front of my face so that I wanted to scream, but I could still kick him away, right? Lock my arms against his chest, keep my mouth closed so nothing dripped in it.

All of which would have happened, too.

Except for Les.

He'd picked up the bat that I guess I'd dragged through the chalk between second and third, so that, when he slapped it into the side of Michael T's head, a puff of white kind of breathed up. At first I thought it was bone, powdered skull—the whole top of Michael T's rotted-out head *was* coming off—but then there was sunlight above me again, and Les was hauling me up, and, on the sidewalk, Amber Watson was just staring at me, her whistle still in her mouth, her hair still wet enough to have left a dark patch on the canvas of the sneakers looped over her shoulder.

I put two of my fingers to my eyebrow like I'd seen my dad do, launched them off in salute to her, and in return she shook her head in disappointment. At the kid I still obviously was. So, yeah, if you want to know what it's like living with zombies, this is it, pretty much: they mess everything up. And if you want to know why I never went pro, it's because I got in the habit of charging the mound too much, like I had all this momentum from that day, all this unfairness built up inside. And if you want to know about Amber Watson, ask Les Moore—that's his real, stupid name, yeah. After that day he saved my life, became the real Indian because *he'd* been the one to scalp Michael T, he stopped coming to the diamond so much, started spending more time at the pool, his hair bleaching in the sun, his reflexes gone, always thirty-five cents in his trunks to buy a lifeguard a lemonade if she wanted.

And she did, she does.

And, me? Some nights I still go to the old park, spiral up to the top of the rocket with a 'Bury the Tomahawk' or 'Circle the Wagons' spirit ribbon, and I let it flutter a bit through the grimy bars before letting it go, down through space, down to the planet I used to know, miles and miles from here.

BECAUSE MY THERAPIST ASKED ME TO TELL A STORY USING HAMSTERS

Bedtime in the cage.

Our Mommy Hamster would sit in the hall between my sister's wire room and my wire room and read us wonderful stories. We could see her just a little, sitting there in the chair she'd dragged over, and we would lie at the edge of our beds facing the door, making sure she hadn't scampered away to the dishes or the food bowl or to her bed of newspaper.

Sometimes too, through the walls we could see the shape of our Father Hamster, walking on all fours, smelling of each thing and then whipping his face away, disgusted. But coming back to smell again and again.

It was our Mommy Hamster's voice that carried us into sleep each night, though. The last thing we'd see would be her fuzzy, backlit shape in her chair. On the best nights, we could stay awake long enough for her to fall asleep as well, the corner of her book gnawed into a soggy mess. Then, every time the cage rattled and we shook awake, there she'd be in her same place, and we could go back to sleep again, because the world was all right.

But, as she told us each night before reading, she had a lot of stuff to do before bedding down herself. And when she said it, her whiskers would flick back towards the living room, giving away the source of her twitchy nerves: Father.

She wouldn't tell us the story, but we knew from an aunt that when we were born, Father had tried to eat us.

If we ever told Mommy we knew this, she would have just hushed us, told us that it was all a big misunderstanding. That that's not the way daddies act, is it?

So of course we never told her. It would have hurt, to hear her have to lie.

And, even though the plea was there in her voice each night, for us to go to sleep early this time, so she could do her chores, still, her voice, we never wanted to let it go.

We don't blame her is what I'm trying to say.

What she did, finally, was when we'd start to nod off while she was reading, just our nose moving but to no place in particular, she'd take one of her old jackets, a few armfuls of loose paper from the corner, and some of the colored string that had been dropped down through the ceiling for us to play with, and fashion a surrogate for herself. A dummy Mommy. One that, our eyes still thick with sleep, and the lights off anyway, the only sound Father working the ball in the drinking tube, we could mistake for her. Or not question before falling back to sleep anyway.

The weeks after she started doing that, we slept better than ever, like we were curled around ourselves twice, and then had enough energy that we were chewing up all the papers before Father could even get to them. It was a dream. And Mommy even lost that frantic look around her eyes, a little. She was finally getting to the dishes, the bedding, all the things she needed to do but never had been able to.

It was the perfect solution.

Until we found the dummy Mommy in the hall closet.

But we loved her, too, the real one, were beginning to have a sense of what she was going through in the cage night after night, day after day, week after week. So we allowed the charade to continue. Each night while she read, we would chant to ourselves in our head, either that it was the dummy Mommy reading, and that that was all right (just don't think about the mouth), or, if that wasn't working, we'd pray that when we woke in the night, we'd have forgotten that it wasn't really her sitting there.

Like all good games of pretend, though, there came a night where . . . where—

What happened, and I've never told my sister this, because I love her too, but what happened is that I woke. Not from a sound, but a sense. It was Father. He was creeping along the wall in the next room, his nose to the corner, following it like a rat.

Through the wire wall I could only see his general outline, but it was enough for me to know the look he had on his face.

It was the same one I'd imagined a hundred times, the same I knew he'd had the day we were born.

But it was okay, it was okay. We weren't furless pups anymore. The instinct had to be drained out of him, right?

Somewhat.

He wasn't after us was the thing.

I settled my eyes on Mommy Hamster just as he got to her, just as he stood on his hind legs, his forepaws clamped onto her dry shoulder, his pelvis thrusting over and over into—the side of her head? Her ear?

And she just took it, and took it, and then I remembered: it was a thing of straw he was abusing, a dummy made from string, made to take her place.

I smiled.

Two floors up, through the wire so that she was just the dimmest of shadows, I could see our Mommy Hamster.

She had paused for a moment in the mouth of one of the great tubes that went forever away. Paused to check the air, to check on us.

"Go," I whispered to her in my loudest quiet voice, "run away," and, slowly at first but then faster and faster, so that her claws were clacking on the plastic, she did.

THE CALORIE DOCTOR

The therapist I find in the yellow pages tells me both that I'm overweight—the obvious, why I'm there in his office in the first place—and that overweight people, while not quite schizophrenic, seem nevertheless to be touched by it, as, since they're unable to accept that the person who sits down to this big meal is the same person who's going to wear that meal around their middle, they must in some essential way be two people, at which point he makes the standard joke about those amazing weight-loss stories and the associated visuals— the pants two people could fit into, sit in like a hot tub—but that's anecdotal, not really support for his schizophrenia argument. What is is that later, when I'm field dressing him on his mahogany desk, both of us medicated (him with anesthetic from his locked drawer, me with appetite), he's still trying to make his point, explain to me how his offhand observation about two people in one body was my trigger, my psychotic break—this his words essentially gave me license to 'feed' (his word) my other, gluttonous self, the one who's going to have to deal with this meal, and that both of me should understand that none of this is our fault, but his, an elaborate suicide, 'obesity kills,' ha ha, and I smile, pull a string of meat from his between his surprisingly shiny ribs, hold it up to the bare bulb of his expensive lamp, to check for marbling, and ask him who's dissociative now?

STORY NOTES

GOOD TIMES

If I were a better person, I wouldn't have written this story. Or I would have deleted it. But alas.

THE AGE OF HASTY RETREATS

This is the middle section of a story *Weird Tales* published, "Notes from the Apocalypse." It's somehow the heart of that story, though. You know how some people will write a fantasy story just to see a unicorn? I think I wrote this one just to get a better look at that 'progenitor'-guy, with bandolier kittens.

MY HERO

I used to work in Book Cataloging at a university library, which had a lot of cubicles. That's where and why I wrote this story. Really, back then I wrote a lot of office stories. It was such a cool place, and there were just stories all around, and I found myself, like Vigilante Man, always getting carried away, always making things more meaningful via secret identities and distant pleas for help. I didn't do my job just exceedingly well, but I did write a whole, whole lot. Which is my real job, of course.

HOW BILLY HANSON DESTROYED THE PLANET EARTH, AND EVERYONE ON IT

This is maybe my longest title to date. Either it or "The Complete Silence of Cats is Another Definition for Silence." And, I wrote this because I wanted to see if you could actually use stars' gravity to look through like a tunnel. Turns out you can, but you shouldn't. That seems to be the story a lot of the time, really.

LITTLE MONSTERS

Paul Tremblay and John Langan hit me up for a monster story for their *Creatures* anthology, and I told them sure, then forgot about it until the last possible instant. So I sat down, tried to see what a monster was made of in the forty-five minutes I had left. Turns out they're made of love and tenderness and regret and nostalgia and hope. Who'd have guessed.

THE HALF LIFE OF PARENTS

The first time I wrote this, that young couple's kid dies, and then it ends with muppets. Or hand puppets. But my agent and a friend both told me that was stupid. And, I like it better like this, finally, after so many versions. As for where it comes from: my dad gave my kids a VHS of some old half-cartoon *Beany and Cecil*, and it's completely and permanently freaked me out. Even just to think about. It's a cartoon, but there's this live-action hand-puppet in the background. Which I just cannot process. Thus, this story. Stories are always me trying to make sense of the world. Because the world's sure not doing it on its own.

OLD MEAT

Finding the delivery method for this story was a trick. I had to take a few runs at it. But then I read somewhere about the origins of that old hook-hand story, and I knew this was a help-column letter. And, everybody writes about werewolves in their prime, yes? What about the golden years, though? What's left then? Love, devotion, and a terror so abject that you shiver inside. It's wonderful, I mean. It has to be. I can't wait.

NEARER TO THEE

I started into this one thinking it'd be cool to play with names so as to foretoken a re-disaster. But then all the gameshow trivia presented itself, completely on accident—the character had to have some mechanism for recognizing this. This story and the "Billy Hanson" one go hand-in-hand, for me. And they're each just trying to burrow inside Arthur C. Clarke's "The Nine Billion Names of God," of course. Trying to burrow inside and live.

JUMPERS

I wrote this right around the same time as "My Hero." There's also a third in this series, "Amateur Hour," the longest of the three, and probably indebted to a *Seinfeld* episode. This one, however, owes itself largely to Harlan Ellison's "The Man Who Rowed Christopher Columbus Ashore." Hopefully obviously, but not quite illegally. Hey, Harlan.

THE SEA OF INTRANQUILITY

I never sit down with the purpose of writing something way on the edge of the real. Except this time. Court Merrigan hit me up for his Pulp issue of *Pank*, and just told me to surprise him, pretty much. To see what I could do if not just the blinders were pulled away, but the eyeballs too. The eyeballs with stems. This is that story. What surprised me too was that, once I wrote the first line, the whole story seemed to be already there in my head. I just had to race to get it all down right. Took maybe two hours?

THIS IS NOT WHAT I MEANT

I wrote this while working the warehouse at Sears. 2000, 2001? I was still, of necessity, moonlighting from being a professor. I couldn't decide which I was going to stick with, either. And, that warehouse, it was a freaktacular place, definitely. Each morning I'd wake at five, be the first person on the streets of Lubbock, and they'd all be dusted white with mosquito poison. Driving through it was like being in a snow globe, or the apocalypse.

And then the warehouse, where we were all automatons, occasionally losing it and becoming so, so human all at once. So much stuff was stolen, so many jobs lost, so many people laying open-eyed on the shelves with the microwaves and air conditioners, hiding. This story is that hiding. I spent a lot of time on a certain shelf, pretending I was a box.

THE CASE AGAINST HUMANITY

I half-suspect this is the core of everything I write. It feels true to me. It's undisguised, it's naked, it's bare. And ~~they~~ we all deserve it.

HELL ON THE HOMEFRONT TOO

This is my official first zombie story ever. And my only TG Sheppard story (so far—guy's good). I didn't write it for the zombie in it, though. I wrote it because I wanted to have a character named "Letch," and because I'd been listening for days to "The Night the Lights Went Out in Georgia." Just over and over and over. That song cycles through my life, takes me over like that every few years, where it's the only thing I can listen to. Because I can't understand it—I can't understand why the narrator's telling us all this, and what her method for selection is. But it's all perfect, too.

I WAS A TEENAGE SLASHER VICTIM

In trying to figure out how it is that Jason Voorhees and that crowd are always so strong, I wrote this story. Stories are the only way I can ever figure anything out. Future-muscles, though. It all makes sense now. And, I have another "I Was a Teenage _____" story I've been carrying in my hip pocket for nearly twenty years now. Waiting for it to ripen. In waiting, though, I burned its key line (in "Sea of Intranquility"). No matter, though. Good stories generate their own killer lines.

THE MANY STAGES OF GRIEF

Another story that comes from cubicle-land. Also, I guess I should say that, of every story and novel I've ever written, even *The Long Trial of Nolan Dugatti*, which I did in seventy-two hours, so had no time to hide, this is the most honest. This is the one where the main character is me, without any hiding at all. Not even a little. This was the year I was writing all true stories, just with different facts (another: "Hemingway Hills in the Afternoon"). As for why I wrote this: one of my brothers had a friend named Tad. And that always kind of freaked me out for reasons I couldn't quite track. Like, I'd just get very nervous even hearing a story about him, like—*can't everybody else tell what's wrong, here?* Evidently not. So I wrote this, trying to figure it out. Turns out it was me who was wrong here.

CATCH AND RELEASE

Man, I don't know why I write about aliens so much. Blame Whitley Strieber. Blame Chris Carter. Blame this one tabloid I found under the stairs of a half-built house we moved into, a magazine I arranged black widows and wasps and candles and stolen rings and stuff around, and made myself sit with for certain long periods of time, and then sheetrocked that little not-a-room over, so that ritual is still going, thirty-five years later. Or, yes, though this story can't hope to even approach him, blame Terry Bisson. Of all the stories I've done that are all dialogue, this is one of two that I think halfway match up with what I was initially hearing in my head. The other is "The Broaching." And I never opened that magazine under the stairs, either. It had a guy on front that, looking from now, might have been Max Headroom. Then, though, he was an alien, and this was the only copy of that magazine, and I was terrified and thrilled and forever changed.

SUBMITTED FOR YOUR APPROVAL

Twilight Zone was just as important to the twentieth century as Einstein and Freud, I think. Or, Serling, he's part of that trinity. What he gave us, it changed us forever, and in the best ways. And, it's not knowing our minds or knowing the math of the world that's going to save us, finally. It's being able to dream ourselves into something else, something different. I can't wait.

DEATHTRAP WHIRLPOOL

I have two constant fears. One is that I'm driving somewhere and look down and there's no key in the ignition, meaning none of this is real, and the other is that I'm an unwitting contestant on a future gameshow. That second is a function of narcissism, I know, and I guess I should apologize for it. But it might be true, too. Everything might depend on whether I open the door now, or after I've counted to four in a certain way. It's a terrible weight to carry. Somebody's got to, though.

ZOMBIE SHARKS WITH METAL TEETH

I wrote this, man, ten years ago, now? And, just two days ago, I wrote another story kind of walking the paces of a different set of scientific . . . principles, theories, investigations, maybes. This guy in here, his brain and my brain, they're one brain. And sometimes they're unfolding at a rate it's a trick to try to track. Best I can do is write, and write faster, like if I scratch that paper deep enough, it's finally going to whisper all the secrets of the world to me.

ROCKET MAN

Everybody's always worried about zombies eating you. But what if they also managed to lose you your girlfriend? The one who's not even your actual girlfriend, but the love of your life, only she doesn't know it yet? *There's* some horror. Affairs of the heart always trump your insides being on the outside. And, some of you might notice that the playground rocket in this—dude's done that before. Sorry? It's just that it's one of the touchstones of my growing up. Every time I'd run away, I always came back to that rocket in Stanton, Texas. It was always there for me, ready to take me wherever I needed to go. Thanks, rocket. I'll be back soon.

BECAUSE MY THERAPIST ASKED ME TO TELL A STORY USING HAMSTERS

I think I wrote this while reading Alison Bechdel's *Fun Home*. And I mixed it with the dad-in-disguise therapist from *Infinite*

Jest. Just, the idea of talking to a therapist, it's always kind of freaked me out. I'm sure they do good and necessary stuff, but—it's why I never go on stage to get hypnotized: I'm fairly certain I would never be the same person afterward. Which, I mean, that might be better, I'm not saying it wouldn't. But we hold on tight to what we know, too. At least I do. The reason I eat only glazed donuts, it's that I ate one once, way back, and knew it was perfect, and I didn't need to try any others, however so long I shall live.

THE CALORIE DOCTOR

This came from some ad I heard on the radio, I think. About losing weight. And I thought, man, this is a violent, violent world we live in. So I did what I could to document that a little.

ACKNOWLEDGMENTS

Thanks to John Wang, who published a few of these at *Juked* over the years. Thanks to Court Merrigan, for prompting me to write one of them, and to Paul Tremblay and John Langan, who got me to write another. Thanks to a guy named Herb, for driving a purple bus once. I'm still waiting for that bus to come over the horizon one more time, Herb. Thanks to Jeremy Robert Johnson. For that amazing introduction, but he's also the reason for some of these. You see somebody firing on all cylinders, and you want to go that fast too. Carlton Mellick III challenges me in the same way: I see what he's doing on the page, and I think *Would it be safe to go farther? Is it even possible?* Not really. But it's fun to try. Same with Vonnegut: I'll never be him, but I guess nobody else will be either. Doesn't stop us all from dressing up in his cast-offs, though. Thanks to Cameron Pierce, for bringing me into Lazy Fascist, the original publisher of this book, for, now, three books. If not for him, *Zombie Sharks with Metal Teeth* wouldn't have even been an idea. I mean, I knew I had this one directory of stories that were always oozing out over the fences, peering back over with their stalk-eyes and grinning goodbye in their secret evil ways, but, until Cameron hit me up to collect them, I never knew what they could look like all in place. And, thanks to Cameron for titling this one, too. My title was, as is often the case, stupid. Working with good people, though, I've had the luxury of getting to be stupid, as there's always someone there to catch me. Thanks to Diane Hueter Warner, for hiring me into a book cataloging unit once upon a time. A lot of these not only come from there, they were also written there. Thanks to Janet Burroway. The first of these stories, I wrote it for your workshop back in 1997, I think. And I still remember the silence of nobody having any idea what to say that wouldn't either hurt my feelings or show that they had no idea what had just happened. Don't feel bad; I had no idea either. And thanks to my wife Nancy. No matter how far these stories go, you're there to take my hand, bring me back again. I can't always speak proper words upon re-entry, but you don't make me, either. Let's watch some more *Matlock*, now. Let's do that forever, please.

ABOUT THE AUTHOR

Stephen Graham Jones is the *New York Times*–bestselling author of more than forty novels, collections, novellas, and comic books, including *The Only Good Indians* and the Indian Lake Trilogy. Jones received a National Endowment for the Arts fellowship and has won honors ranging from the Mark Twain American Voice in Literature Award to the Bram Stoker Award. Jones lives and teaches in Boulder, Colorado. Visit his website at stephengrahamjones.com.

STEPHEN GRAHAM JONES

FROM OPEN ROAD MEDIA

OPEN ROAD

INTEGRATED MEDIA

Find a full list of our authors and
titles at www.openroadmedia.com

FOLLOW US
@OpenRoadMedia